CW00868386

Marjorie Dean I

Hamilton Colony

Josephine Chase

Alpha Editions

This edition published in 2022

ISBN : 9789356785861

Design and Setting By
Alpha Editions
www.alphaedis.com
Email - info@alphaedis.com

As per information held with us this book is in Public Domain.
This book is a reproduction of an important historical work. Alpha Editions uses the
best technology to reproduce historical work in the same manner it was first
published to preserve its original nature. Any marks or number seen are left
intentionally to preserve its true form.

Contents

CHAPTER I

"Something fine is going to happen, Bean."

Jerry Macy leaned back in the roomy porch rocker, half-closed blue eyes squinting prophetically up at the turquoise August sky. "Yes, sir; it is."

"Several fine things *ought* to happen, but they haven't." Marjorie Dean Macy's emphasis upon the "ought" was energetically wistful.

"Something celostrous is coming this way," Jerry continued to maintain. "It's in the air."

"I wish it would hurry up, and come, then. Captain was to be home from the beach yesterday. *She* hasn't happened. Leila owes me a letter. *That* hasn't happened yet. I haven't heard from her for over a month, or from Vera, either. And there is Hamilton Arms, still boarded up and with no sign of Miss Susanna, or Jonas. Where is everybody? That's what *I'd* like to know."

"*I'm* with you yet, Mrs. Macy," Jerry reminded pertinently. "And incidentally, you still have a nice kind husband." She beamed upon the lovely occupant of the porch swing with pretended solicitude.

"Thank you for reminding me of my blessings." Marjorie nodded laughing gratitude at Jerry. "What do you *think* is going to happen, wise sooth-sayer?" she asked in the next breath.

"Um-m-m." Jerry's eyes opened a trifle wider. She thrust her dimpled chin forward at a ridiculous angle, peering owlishly about her as though about to pick an answer to Marjorie's question out of the sunlit August air. "Search me," she said after a moment, then giggled.

"*You* are a fake." Marjorie pointed a derisive finger at Jerry.

"Nope. I'm not. I have a pleasant little hunch that we're either going to see somebody we've not expected to see, or else hear from somebody we've not expected to hear from. Now, do you get me, Marjorie Bean Macy?"

"Who, I wonder?" Marjorie said speculatively. "Not Ronny. I used to call her the great unexpected. But I needn't hope, this time, to see her. I received her first honeymoon letter to me only last week. No, Ronny will have to be counted out of your hunch, Jeremiah." Marjorie sighed regretfully. Her affection for Veronica Lynne, her California comrade and chum, was deep-rooted.

"She certainly handed the Travelers the surprise of their lives last June. I'll never forget that last spread in her room on Commencement night, and her calm announcement to us that she was going home to be married to

Professor Leonard in July at the old mission at Mañana. She *was* the great unexpected that night, I'll say. I haven't got over it yet. I never even suspected those two were miles deep in love, and Jeremiah nearly lost her reputation then and there, for knowing something about everything."

"Ronny was always a mystery from the first time I met her playing maid at Miss Archer's. She was always a delightful mystery, too. Somehow, it seemed quite in keeping that she should have given us all such a surprise about Professor Leonard. I'd never even dreamed of Ronny as in love with any man. Perhaps I might have suspected last year how things were between her and Professor Leonard if I hadn't been so dreadfully unsettled in mind about Hal. I doubt it, though. I'm still surprised that you let it get by *you*, Jeremiah."

"And I'm even more surprised that Leila Harper never suspected them as on the brink of love," Jerry returned.

"I'm going to tell you something, Jerry." Marjorie was smiling reminiscently. "I promised Ronny never to tell anyone except you, something she told me just before she left Hamilton, and I was not to tell you until after we'd received her announcement cards."

"Go ahead. Shoot." Jerry sat suddenly straight in her chair, eyes fastened interestedly upon Marjorie's smiling features.

"Ronny never even dreamed Professor Leonard loved her until just before my wedding. They were alone together after classes in the gymnasium on the day before my wedding. They had been talking of Hal and me, and—well—suddenly he began to tell her about himself. His mother was a Spanish Mexican of very good family, and his father met her while he was professor in a Mexican university. Professor Leonard told Ronny that he hoped someday to establish a welfare station and school for poor Mexican children in Mexico. Then quite suddenly he told her how dearly he loved her, but would not ask her to share such a life of sacrifice, and perhaps privation, as his future would undoubtedly hold.

"She'd known for quite a while that she cared for him, but thought he hadn't cared for her in any other than a friendly way. She was so dumbfounded she couldn't say a word at first. He thought he had displeased her, and she had a hard time trying to make him understand that he hadn't; that she truly loved him, and wished more than anything else to marry him and help him carry out his great plan. She never said a word to him about his plan being one of her father's pet dreams, but she wrote her father to come to Hamilton for a flying visit, so as to meet Professor Leonard, and talk with him. He came and stayed in town at the Hamilton house for two days, and, during that time, the three of them came to a perfect understanding of one another. No one except they two knew Mr. Lynne was in Hamilton."

"*Good night!*" Jerry thus vented her astonishment. "I know *one* thing, Ronny would have told you. She'd have included you in that little family confab, too, if you hadn't been up North, on your own honeymoon."

"Yes, she told me she would have," Marjorie admitted, coloring. "But that was only because I was the first friend she made in Sanford, you know."

"Yep. I know. Bing, bang; here goes a new jingle." Jerry raised a declaiming hand and recited:

"Oh glorious Bean, why hide your sheen,

Beneath a bushel's shade.

Your friends all lean on you, good Bean,

On you their hopes are stayed."

"If your jingle were about someone else, I'd praise it as a triumphant inspiration. Since it isn't—you're a ridiculous person, Jeremiah. I think I've told you that before now." Marjorie was regarding Jerry with tolerant amusement. "Kindly repeat that jingle, before you forget it. Oh, yes, and wait until I go for a pencil and paper. I promised Leila faithfully never to let the fruits of your jingling get by me, complimentary to me, or no."

Laughing, Marjorie sprang from the swing and hurried lightly into the house. She was smiling to herself in pure contentment of spirit as she passed through the reception hall and on into the library. Her new home, to which she had come only two weeks before from a lengthy honeymoon, spent in the Adirondacks, was still a matter of delighted wonder to her. During Hal's and her absence, Mr. and Mrs. Dean had been happily occupied in putting the new home of the happy pair to rights, against the day when they should turn their faces toward Hamilton Estates.

Readers of the MARJORIE DEAN HIGH SCHOOL, COLLEGE and POST GRADUATE SERIES can already claim Marjorie and her intimate girl-associates as old friends. They have followed the fortunes of this particular band of devoted chums through both bright and stormy days.

MARJORIE DEAN MACY saw the happy culmination of the romance between Marjorie and Hal Macy in her marriage to him, on a balmy May Day evening at Hamilton Arms, the home of her friend, Miss Susanna Hamilton.

It was now the last of August. Marjorie and Hal had taken possession of their new home the middle of August in order to see Mr. and Mrs. Dean off for a two weeks' stay at their old standby, Severn Beach. Jerry Macy, deep in preparations for her marriage to Danny Seabrooke to take place on the eighth of September, had been unable to resist Marjorie's affectionate invitation to come to her and Hal's new home as the first guest to enter the hospitable portals of "Travelers' Rest."

"I've been here over a week, Mrs. M. D. Macy," she announced as Marjorie returned to the veranda with a pencil and small leather note book. "I simply must hit the trail for Sanford, not later than day after tomorrow. Danny'll think I've lost interest in the marriage idea, and quit him cold."

"I know you *ought* to go," Marjorie nodded. "I've loved having you here with Hal and me."

"You might have a worse sister-in-law," Jerry pointed out with a sly grin.

"I couldn't have a better one. I know that," came with quick loyalty from Marjorie. "What a lot of wonderful things have happened to the Big Six since they paraded home from high school together in good old Sanford."

"Um-m-m. I should say there had. But, do you know, Marjorie, I used to hope, back in those days that some day you'd marry Hal, and become my sister-in-law. After we entered Hamilton and you seemed to care nothing at all for him, except as a friend, it made me feel blue as sixty, at times. Honestly, I never believed then you would finally wake up and fall in love with him." Jerry's chubby features grew reminiscently solemn.

"I wonder now that I could have been so hard-hearted," Marjorie made frank reply. "How could I have hurt Hal so deeply? That's what I ask myself sometimes in the midst of the happiness his love has brought me. I can understand now how Brooke Hamilton must have grieved over Angela. It was his diary that woke me up. And to think! I almost missed love." Marjorie was looking very sober herself.

"Here we sit, solemn as two owls, talking about what didn't happen, thank goodness." Jerry's roguish smile crinkled her lips. "While we're on the subject, I'll tell you a secret. It was the way you turned Hal down that started me to thinking seriously about Danny. I'd always liked Danny a whole lot, but, somehow, I could never take him seriously. Whenever he'd show signs of growing serious, I'd laugh at him. Finally, when you and Hal flivvered, it worried both Danny and me. We did manage one or two serious talks about that. It drew us closer together in sympathy, somehow, and the night we went sailing in the *Oriole*, you remember that night, I realized that he meant a great deal more to me than I'd believed he could. That very night, while we were at the wheel together, I fell in love with him. And you're the first person I ever told it to, and you'll be the last. Believe me, I never let him suspect it, though, until a whole year later."

"I'm highly honored, Jeremiah." Marjorie's words held fond appreciation. "I'm so glad you wished me to know about you and Danny. Frankly, I'd often wondered when and how you and he came to an understanding. You're such a secretive old dear. I used to imagine you didn't care the least little bit about Danny. I was sure he cared for you, though."

"I wasn't sure," Jerry made blunt response. "I mean, not until that summer we were at Severn Beach." Jerry became silent, an absent gleam springing into her merry blue eyes. "And I'm going home day after tomorrow to get ready to be married to Dan-yell," she suddenly broke out with a half humorous inflection. "Can you beat that?"

"No, I can't." Marjorie shook a smiling head. "I think it's———"

"There's the mail man!" Jerry sang out, the absent gleam in her eyes changing to one of eager expectation. "Come on." She sprang up from her chair, and ran down the steps, waving a beckoning arm to Marjorie.

The porch swing rocked wildly as Marjorie left it in a quick rush after Jerry. The pair raced down the wide stone walk to the high arched stone gateway, bringing up, laughing, beside the mail box, fastened to a post, just inside the entrance gates.

"Oh, bother! I forgot the key!" Marjorie exclaimed in mild vexation.

"I have it. I brought it out on the veranda with me. Kindly recall that I've been expecting a love letter from my intended," she reminded, chuckling. "I got ready to grab it." She fished the little key from a diminutive, lace-trimmed pocket of her frock.

"You're a life-saver," Marjorie sighed relief.

Jerry had already busied herself with fitting the key to the lock. "*Great guns!*" she ejaculated, as she swung open the little door of the box. "*Some mail.*"

There were eleven letters, according to her pleasantly-excited count.

"Seven for you, two for old Hal, and three for me," she announced, handing Marjorie her letters and Hal's. "One of mine is from Mother. I'll say it's a 'Why don't you come home, Jerry,' message. One's from Ronny. It's high time she wrote me. This one's from Muriel Harding, and it's postmarked 'New York.' Now what the dickens is she doing in New York? I thought she was at Severn Beach. Curiosity wins. I'll read hers first."

Jerry conducted this lively monologue as she hastily tore open an end of the envelope addressed in Muriel Harding's familiar swinging hand. She extracted the letter from the envelope, glanced quickly down the first page, then gave a funny little shout of surprise.

"Catch me," she implored. "I'm going to drop dead of surprise. Muriel Harding, *you rascal. I told* you something was going to happen, Bean. Well, has it happened? I guess, yes."

CHAPTER II

A JOLT FOR LESLIE

"What is it? Hurry up, and tell me." Marjorie gave Jerry's arm a playfully impatient little shake, her own letters for the moment forgotten.

"Listen to this," Jerry began.

"DEAR OLD JEREMIAH:

"When you read this letter I shall be Mrs. Harry Lenox, and on my way with Harry to South America. Some little jolt, Jeremiah, but you'll survive it. Harry's father, now Muriel's highly-respected papa-in-law, has important business interests in the Argentine. It was impossible for him to make the trip to the Argentine at present, so Harry had to fall in line. That meant he would not return to Sanford until next summer. Poor Muriel. She had grown so used to having Harry around. As you know, we expected to be married in November. Harry said, 'Why not now?' I said, 'It does seem as though something ought to be done about it.' And that's what it's all about.

"Father and Mother went to New York with us, and we were married in the parsonage of St. Andrew's Episcopal Church last Monday afternoon, August twenty-fifth. Don't forget the date. I was married in the ducky pale tan traveling ensemble that I had had made for my November going-away gown. I hadn't yet decided upon my wedding dress, and it was a good thing.

"I'm not yet over my own surprise at the sudden way all my nice, artistic wedding plans went up in the air. One thing, however, I insisted upon—a great big wedding cake. You and Marjorie, and all my other good little pals, will receive a piece of that glorious cake by parcel post.

"It seems awfully strange to be hurrying away from the good old U. S., adventure-bound. I'd always planned a wonderful wedding, with the big Sanford Six strictly on the job. Love is really a serious matter. There could be only one thing more serious, to me—not to be in love.

"I can't stop to write any more just now. It is almost ten o'clock, and we have to be on board the steamer by eleven.

We are to sail for Buenos Aires on the *Maraquita* at midnight. There's no use in trying to tell you how sorry I am about going so far away without having you and the girls on hand to wish me *bon voyage*. You and Marjorie, my dear comrades of years, can understand, above all others, just how I feel about it. I'll write you a long letter as soon as I'm settled on shipboard. Be good, Jeremiah, and remember me to Dan-yell. More about everything then, including several pages of regrets at not being able to join your bridesmaid line on the fateful eighth of September. Oceans of love. You'll hear from me again soon.

"Hastily,

"MURIEL."

"*What* do you think of that?" Jerry's tone conveyed her own feelings. "Muriel was right about the jolt. After all, it's just about what one might expect of Muriel Harding. Maybe I shan't miss her, though. We'd planned a lot of things to do in Sanford next winter." She vented a long, regretful sigh.

"Your hunch came true, Jeremiah. We hadn't expected to hear from Muriel Harding Lenox, in New York, and all ready to sail for South America. You're the only one of the Big Six still single. And your fate is sealed. Four of us are married to the boys who were our high school cavaliers. You're going to marry yours. Susan Atwell is the only one of us who has loved and married far away from Sanford." Marjorie's lovely features had grown dreamily reminiscent.

"There's no use in denying it. We're getting old, Bean; getting old." Jerry gave an elaborately disconsolate sniffle.

It set both chums to giggling as whole-heartedly as in the days when they were freshmen at Sanford High, with the future a closed book, the pages of which neither was curious to scan.

"I've a letter here from Muriel, too," Marjorie said. "Let's go back to the veranda and have a letter-reading bee. One of mine is from Leslie Cairns," Marjorie was busily going over the envelopes in her hand, "and this one's from Robin Page. This one looks like a high-class advertisement. Oh, here's one from Gussie Forbes, postmarked California. Then I've a Paris one from Connie, and last and best one from General. That means he and Captain aren't coming home just yet. Hurry up, Jerry." She began to tow Jerry speedily up the walk to the house. "I'm in a grand rush to begin the bee."

Marjorie laid the two letters for Hal on the willow porch stand, hurriedly returning to the swing, there to enjoy her own. Jerry had plumped down again in her rocker and was already perusing her mother's letter. "What did I tell you?" she commented to Marjorie as she continued to read. "Mother is worrying like mad because I'm lingering longer here than becomes the station of one, Jerry Macy, about to be wed. It's time for me to hit the home plate. I can see that."

"Never mind. We'll all be together again soon," Marjorie reminded.

"And that rascal, Muriel Harding was to have been my maid of honor," Jerry groaned. "Why can't you be my matron of honor, since she's left me in the lurch. I'd rather have you as a first aid to the altar than anyone else." She turned coaxingly to Marjorie.

"I'd love to be, except for one thing. I'd rather stand aside in favor of the unmarried girls," Marjorie said simply. "Let me see. You're going to have Leila, Vera, Leslie, Lucy, Helen Trent and Robin Page as your bridesmaids." She wrinkled her dark brows in a reflective frown. After a moment's silence she spoke: "Jerry, why don't you have Lucy as your maid of honor? Next to the Big Six, she's really nearest to us all. It would make her wonderfully happy."

"Luciferous?" Jerry eyed Marjorie with a contemplative squint. "I never thought of her. I was thinking just this minute that I might ask Helen Trent to take Muriel's place. Helen was my first Hamilton chum, you know. Lucy——" Jerry became suddenly silent. "Right, as usual, beneficent Bean." She nodded conclusively. "I ought to ask Lucy to be my maid of honor. I'll do it, too. Mother says in her letter that the girls' gowns are finished, and waiting for a grand try-on. Lucy's will have to be altered, though. She's considerably shorter than Muriel."

"You haven't told me about the dresses yet, Jeremiah," Marjorie dimpled as she made ingratiating reminder. Thus far Jerry had declined to give details. "I'm going to give you a treat, Bean, so don't ask questions," had been her reply.

"And I'm not going to, either," Jerry came back with her tantalizing grin. "I'll invite you to the try-on. Curb your curiosity till then, or I'll compose a jingle about it," she now threatened.

"You're awfully mean," Marjorie's amused tone belied her words.

"Don't you want to be delightfully surprised?" Jerry demanded.

"Of course I do. I was only funning, my dear Miss Macy."

"Glad to hear it. I'd hate to hurt your feelings, Mrs. Macy."

"Don't mention it. There ain't no such animal," Marjorie retorted.

Smilingly, the two friends again went back to their letters. Jerry was soon lost in the many pages of Ronny's long friendly message. Marjorie was finding equal pleasure in a long letter from Constance Armitage. Every now and then, one of the pair would read aloud a particular paragraph of her letter for the edification of the other.

Jerry had finished Ronny's letter before Marjorie had come to the end of the one from Constance. She busied herself with a rereading of Muriel's, smiling broadly to herself over it.

Marjorie was also smiling, as though she had suddenly come into the knowledge of an extremely pleasant secret. The affectionate sidelong glance she shot at Jerry seemed to indicate that it strictly concerned the latter.

Presently she took up the letter from Leslie Cairns. It was hardly more than a note, phrased in Leslie's pithy fashion.

> "Dearest Bean," it began. "September's near, and I'm glad of it. I've tried Newport, the Catskills, and various other lady-like resorts just to please Mrs. Gaylord, who is on the job, keeping an eye on Cairns II while Peter is carrying on a snappy financial war with the wolf pack in London. We're home in little old New York now, and Hamilton will be my next stop. Have you a night's lodging for a weary Traveler, should the spirit move me to drop down, just like that, upon you? Gaylord is so full of plans concerning what she ought to do, may do, and intends to do, next, she doesn't know where she's at. I hope she decides to visit her relatives, *pronto*. I can then gracefully kiss her good-bye, and beat it for Hamilton. I suppose the campus is looking as lively just now as a ten-acre lot after a circus has moved off it. Nothing doing there yet. What? I'm going to descend on Remson, and good old Fifteen again, though Peter hopes we'll be housed at Carden Hedge by Christmas. I have a new car. It's some speedy flash. I let it out the other day for Gaylord's benefit. She almost lost her breath, and her confidence in Leslie is now missing. What's the use in trying to write the news? I'd rather tell it to you. You may expect me. Love, as per usual, dear Bean.

"Faithfully (but bored to a frazzle),

"LESLIE."

"Listen to Leslie's funny letter," Marjorie commanded.

"I'm listening." Raising her head from her own letters, Jerry's eyes strayed toward the pike. With a quick exclamation she sprang to her feet. "Look!" she cried, and rushed across the lawn to the drive.

One swift glance, and Marjorie had dashed down the steps in Jerry's wake. A station taxicab was just turning into the drive through the open gates. She gave a jubilant little shout as she glimpsed a laughing face peering out of an open window of the tonneau, and re-doubled her pace.

"Leila!" Her voice rose to a happy staccato. "You dear, precious old fake. Whoever would have thought of seeing *you* today. No wonder I haven't heard from you." She was at the opened door of the machine now, grabbing enthusiastically at the tall, blued-eyed Irish girl just emerging from the car.

"It is myself, and none other." Leila was out of the car now, clinging affectionately to Marjorie. "Ah, Beauty, you are a rare sight to a poor Irish emigrant."

"Where's emigrant number two?" Jerry had come up and joined in the embracing. She peered past Leila into the tonneau of the car.

"Right here," came in prompt tones. Vera Mason's charming blonde head poked itself into view. She sprang from the car, laughing, a dainty, diminutive figure in her smart gray traveling coat and tight little felt hat.

She was immediately seized and hugged, Marjorie and Jerry exclaiming over the welcome pair, girl fashion. Jerry's quick eyes had caught sight of a third occupant of the tonneau. The latter, sat huddled in the far corner of the broad seat, face obscured by the folds of a silk scarf, carefully draped over it.

"You can't fool *me*. Come out, *pronto*, and give an account of yourself," Jerry commanded. Making an agile reach into the tonneau she snatched the concealing scarf from the wearer's face, revealing Leslie Cairns' rugged laughing features.

"How are you, Macy?" Leslie made an attempt at a tone of calm nonchalance which ended in a hearty burst of laughter.

"Fine and dandy, Cairns II," Jerry caught Leslie's extended hands and began dragging her out of the car.

"Steady, there. You certainly have strong-arm methods." Leslie came out of the car with a bounce, due to Jerry's forceful assistance.

"*Why, Leslie!*" Marjorie's brown eyes were wide with pleasant astonishment. "You, too! How splendid. I had just finished reading your letter when Jerry saw the taxi turning in at our gate."

"Gaylord went, and I came. Wait a minute. This taxi man thinks he's been held up here for an hour." Leslie paid the fidgeting driver, who had already placed the travelers' luggage on the drive.

Jerry picked up two of the bags. "More of my strong-arm methods," she observed.

"I'll take Vera's, and mine," Leslie reached for them.

"Since they seem to love work, why should we interfere?" Leila remarked innocently.

"Why, indeed," Marjorie gaily agreed.

She and Leila led the way to the house, arms about each other's waists, talking animatedly as they walked.

"Welcome, Travelers," she called out as they entered the large square living room. She turned, arms outspread, with a pretty gesture of hospitality. "What does this room remind you of?" she turned to Vera and Leila. She burst into a merry little laugh as a big, gray and white Angora cat sat up, yawning widely, in a deep-cushioned chair. "You old fluffy give-away!" she exclaimed.

"Castle Dean!" both girls cried in concert. "Ruffle!"

"And it's plain to be seen a good household fairy whisked the castle here from Sanford, Ruffle puss, and all," Leila declared with an enthusiastic touch of brogue and a fond dive at Ruffle. "The top of the afternoon to you, Ruffle Claws." She swept down upon Ruffle, gathering him, struggling, into her arms.

"Now, now, now, is this the way to behave? I see you have the same old claws. Have you no welcome, then, for Irish Leila?"

"Nu-u-u." Ruffle accompanied his loud protest with a wild scramble out of Leila's prisoning arms. He sprang for his chair, regaining it, and spreading out in it with an air of lofty defiance.

"Never mind. I shall charm you yet with catnip and cunning blarney." Leila shook her finger at the Angora. "This is the room I loved best at Castle Dean," she said to Marjorie. "What good fortune to find it again here."

"We all felt the same about it. Since General and Captain were to make their home ours, and ours, theirs, the four of us got together and decided that we'd better transplant our living room to Hamilton Estates. It forms a link, somehow, between Sanford and here. So many wonderful things have happened in this dear comfy room. *You* never saw it before, Leslie, but you'll soon become well acquainted with it."

Thoughtfulness prompted Marjorie to add this last to her cheery explanation. Despite the fact that she was now on the friendliest of terms with the girls she had once despised, at times Leslie still showed signs of awkward embarrassment when among them.

"I love it already." The oddly somber look, which had briefly touched Leslie's dark features, vanished. "It's the most home-like room I've ever stepped into. I'm home-hungry, you know," she confessed. "I'm going to make a bang-up, homey home for my father at Carden Hedge."

"We shall all be going there to see you, lucky Leslie. It is only poor Midget and I who have no home. Oh, wurra, wurra!" Leila wailed the last two words soulfully.

"Plenty of noise, but no tears," Vera commented slyly.

"She knows me," Leila turned an indicative thumb toward Vera. "Or, it may be she thinks she knows. It is all the same."

"I hope you will all come and hang around the Hedge—a whole lot," Leslie said with half wistful emphasis. "Peter the Great and I are planning to be 'at home' there by Christmas. I'm going to hold my old stand-by, Fifteen, until our new home is ready. I'm undecided regarding P. G. subjects. I'll specialize in something—don't know yet what I want to take up."

"You had best be satisfied with one subject," Leila put in. "It is small time you'll have for more than one after college opens."

Her eyes on Leila, Marjorie read in the Irish girl's tone an odd significance which Leslie had missed.

"I shan't try to mix much in college affairs," Leslie shook a decided head. "I'll have time enough on my hands for three subjects, provided I'm ambitious enough to become a faithful study-hound."

"She says, 'three subjects.' Now what do you think of that, Midget?" Leila stared at Vera in pretended wonder.

"What are you trying to do—kid me?" Leslie's sober features relaxed into a faint smile. Quickly they shadowed again as she said: "You girls can understand why I'm not keen on doing the social side of college. It's best for me to go quietly about my own affairs on the campus." A deep flush had risen to her cheeks. She made an abrupt pause, in itself eloquent of her meaning.

"Oh, shucks!" burst impatiently from Jerry. "You don't know your own worth, Leslie. The social side of Hamilton needs *you*, in particular, to help make things zip. You've already a reputation on the campus——"

"That's just the trouble," Leslie interrupted dryly. "Not the pleasant sort of reputation you mean, Jeremiah. It's the old one—the one that I've not yet succeeded in living down. I hope to do it—in time, by hard, unobtrusive work for Hamilton College. That's the only way it can be done." Her rugged features settled into purposeful lines.

"Do you hear that, Midget? She is that anxious to be hard-working!"

This time Leslie caught the amused exchange of eye-signals between Leila and Vera.

"See here, you two," she challenged, "what's the joke?" For a brief instant a glint of hurt suspicion sprang into her dark eyes. It snapped out as quickly as it had appeared. She said good-humoredly, "Why not tell it to the gang? Then we can all laugh. Is it an Irish joke on Leslie?"

"It is, indeed. Midget and I made it up in Ireland." Leila flashed Leslie a tantalizing smile.

"Well?" Leslie urged expectantly. "Shoot it at me."

"Now I warn you, beforehand, that if you should not like our joke it would be a sorry joke on me," Leila fixed comically-concerned eyes on Leslie.

"I'm already beginning to feel doubtful about it. You'd better shoot," Leslie warningly advised.

"It seems that I had." Leila looked solemnly impressed. "Well, it was this way: One day while Midget and I were wandering around the edge of a deep green bog," Leila began, story fashion, "I said to Midget, 'Does it not seem hard to you that your friend, Leila, should have to write plays and be a theatrical manager, too?' 'It does,' she said. 'I can see you will be in a bog as deep as the one over there when you go back to Hamilton.' 'What a comfort you are to me, Midget,' I said with a deep sigh. 'I have often thought so,' she replied gently."

A funny little treble giggle from Vera broke Leila up in the midst of her recital. She burst out laughing, her companions joining in the wave of mirth that swept the big room.

"Now I have lost the thread of my tale," Leila declared after two or three mirthfully-ineffectual attempts at continuing it. "Where was I at? Ah, yes, I then said to Midget: 'I should be one, or the other, but not both.' She said, 'Quite true, but don't ask me to be the one you decide not to be. I cannot write plays, and it is all I can do to manage my own affairs.' 'Be aisy,' I said with a fine touch of brogue. 'You are not my idea of either.' 'Thank goodness,' she said, not at all peevish. 'I feel that I was intended to be a playwright,' I said. 'I am that temperamental!' 'Something like that,' she said.

'I have no genius for managing,' I confessed. 'I cannot contradict you,' said Midget. 'You had best turn that delicate little job over to someone else who has.'"

Leila paused. Her genial smile flashed broadly into evidence. Her eyes strayed inquiringly to Marjorie.

The latter was leaning forward in her chair, a lovely picture of delighted animation. "Oh, Leila!" she exclaimed. "How perfectly splendid!"

"You have guessed something, Beauty. Was it not good advice that Midget gave me? Now to follow it." Her head made a swift sudden turn from Marjorie to Leslie. "Will you be manager of the Leila Harper Playhouse, Leslie?" she asked practically, then added drolly: "I shall tear my black hair in a fine frenzy if you refuse."

"Why—I—what?" Seated on the davenport Leslie had been leaning far forward, elbows on knees, hands cupping her chin, her eyes fixed on Leila. The unexpected suddenness of Leila's question gave her a veritable jolt. She made a startled forward movement, slid off the edge of the davenport and sat down smartly on the floor.

CHAPTER III

LESLIE AND LEILA

"Can you blame me?" Leslie had finally managed to make herself heard above the gale of laughter that had attended her mishap. She still sat on the floor, regarding her laughing companions with half sheepish reproach.

"No-o," Leila made mirthful answer. "Let us be assisting the new manager to rise, Jeremiah, since we are the strongest of this crowd."

"Thank you. I can assist myself." Leslie sprang to her feet, resuming her former seat on the davenport. "You certainly have handed me a jolt, Leila Harper. It's the last thing I ever thought of."

"Then let it be the first now." There was a vibration of earnestness in Leila's reply. "Summed up in three little words: 'I need you.' There's no other girl on the campus so well-fitted as you for the job. You're a good business person, Leslie. Better still, you're thoroughly cosmopolitan."

"Oh, I don't think so." Flushing at the praise, Leslie shook her head. "It's my self-assured manner that gives me the impression of knowing a whole lot more than I really do," she explained frankly.

"Rubbish!" came energetically from Vera. "You are what you are, Leslie Cairns—clever as—as," she groped mentally for a fitting comparison,—"as Leila."

"Listen to that." Leila made Vera a killingly appreciative bow.

"Nothing like it. I wish I were," Leslie said regretfully.

"Let us have a contest, so that we may learn whether you are more clever than I, or, I than you," Leila proposed blandly. "If you will have pity on a distracted Irish playwright, and help her out, then we shall both be in a fair way to out-do each other in cleverness."

Leila had scented refusal of the honor she wished to do Leslie in the latter's undecided manner. She now proposed to give her no chance to refuse. "We shall have fine times consulting together since we shall be near each other at Wayland Hall," she smoothly pointed out.

"I'd love to manage the Playhouse, and I know Peter the Great would be delighted to have me do it, except for one thing." Leslie spoke in her direct way. "There'd surely be ill-natured criticisms raised about it. Suppose it was said that Peter hadn't been disinterested in giving the Playhouse to Hamilton College; that he had given it with the idea of making me foremost, and important, in campus affairs. Probably more spiteful remarks than that might be circulated."

She stopped, staring half moodily at Leila. "'The way of the transgressor is hard.'" She gave a short mirthless laugh. "Those first three years of mine on the campus were a mess. I behaved like a villain. Now it's up to me to stand the gaff."

"No, Leslie, it isn't." Marjorie cut in decidedly. "You have more than retrieved whatever mistakes you made during your first three years at Hamilton by what you did last year. Leila needs you this year. You would be an ideal manager for the Playhouse. Don't allow anything else to matter. Depend upon it, Leila has already thought up some nice way of arrangement for you. I can see it in that beaming smile of hers."

"I have fine arrangements for all occasions." Leila was now grinning broadly. "When college opens I shall write an article for the 'Campus Echo,'" she continued. "In it I shall outline the policy of the Playhouse, and give a resumé of what I intend to do in the way of plays during the college year. I shall also state that I have asked Leslie to assume the managership of the theatre, because of her extreme capability. Then let anyone start anything, and watch Irish Leila take the field, five feet at a bound, shillalah in hand."

"Give us an imitation now of that five-foot bound," coaxed Jerry.

"Not until I have first practiced it in private," Leila declared with canny firmness. "And I suppose all is now settled, as amiably as you please, and the Playhouse has a new manager." She turned ingratiatingly to Leslie, who could not help smiling, despite her doubts.

"I don't know." Leslie still demurred. "I——" she glanced about her at the little group of friendly, interested faces. She understood that her friends were hoping she might say "yes." "I guess—so," she said uncertainly. "Yes, I'll accept the honor, mostly, though, to please you girls, and—Peter the Great."

"Hurrah, hurray, hurroo!" Leila sent up a jubilant little cheer. "The world shall yet hear of us. Cairns and Harper, the greatest living promoters of high-class campus drama. That is what people will presently be saying about us."

"Nothing succeeds like nerve," Jerry declared.

"And it is experience that teaches the truth of that fine sentiment," Leila came back with an innocent air that raised a general laugh at Jerry's expense.

"I am a most thoughtless and inhospitable hostess!" Marjorie exclaimed as the wave of laughter subsided. "I should have told Delia to make ready a feast, and then——"

"*Delia!*" came in a concerted, delighted shriek from Leila and Vera.

"Of course. How could the Deans and the Macys ever get along without Delia? She's our own, heart and soul."

"Lead us to her," begged Leila. "We're not famished, Beauty. We bumped into Leslie on the train, and the three of us had luncheon together. Ah, but there was a happy pow-wow when we met, subdued and ladylike you may be sure. So it is not Delia's delectable eats, but delectable Delia herself we are bent upon seeing."

"Come along then." Marjorie waved them kitchenward.

The visiting party burst into the kitchen upon Delia who sat placidly in her kitchen rocker shelling peas and humming to herself.

"I knew you'd be askin' right away for me, Miss Leila." Delia sprang up, hastily dumping a lapful of pea shells into a nearby splint basket. She came forward to meet Leila, her face bright with beaming confidence. "I saw you from the kitchen garden when the taxi stopped on the drive. I just thought then how surprised Miss, I mean, Mrs. Macy must be to see you." Delia giggled at her own slip of title. "I can't remember to call Miss Marjorie by her married name," she confessed.

"I'm not quite used myself to my new name," was Marjorie's laughing comment. "Once in a while Jerry calls me Mrs. Macy, but not with proper respect. I'm very fond of my Bean name." She dimpled at Leslie whose answering smile was a mixture of amusement and confusion.

"The tea is ready now, Mrs. Macy. Everything's on the tea wagon in the pantry. I thought you girls would need a little bit to eat until dinner. I was just goin' to wheel the lunch into the livin' room when you come out here. I feel so glad to think you come to see me," Delia looked her pleased pride of the invasion.

"It's here we shall take our tea, in honor of you," Leila said. "I am the one to pour it, and we shall all wait on you."

"Fine." Jerry dashed for the pantry, to return trundling the tea wagon.

Vera was already bowing Delia back into her rocker. "Stay seated most magnificent and highly-esteemed Delia," she directed grandly.

"Te, he, he," Delia chuckled at the flowery encomium.

"Oh, Delia! I forgot you'd never before met Leslie. This is Leslie Cairns, Delia. Leslie shake hands with Delia." Marjorie gaily performed the introduction. "Leslie is going to be our neighbor at Carden Hedge, at Christmas, Delia. Won't that be fine?"

"It will," Delia nodded, all smiles. "The more of Miss Marjorie's friends that come to live near her, the better it is for her. I'm glad to know you, Miss Leslie."

Leslie shook hands warmly with Delia, pleased by the maid's friendly sincerity. She could not help mentally contrasting her present democratic attitude with that of her former snobbish contempt for persons in humbler circumstances than herself. "Cairns II, you're improving," was her whimsical thought. "There's a lot of room yet for improvement, though, so don't get chesty."

The tea party proved to be a hilariously happy event, with Delia the guest of honor, despite her half-abashed, good-natured expostulations.

"I'm going to tear you all away from Delia now," Marjorie finally made firm announcement. "I'm going to see you safely to your own little corners of Travelers' Rest. Then I must come back to the kitchen and help Delia, or you won't have any dinner tonight." She shot Delia a mischievous glance.

"Oh, now, Miss Marjorie——" Delia began. "Jus's though I couldn't get along without Alice. It's Alice's day out," she explained to the newly arrived guests, referring to the absent maid.

"Jerry can keep on playing porter. Only, I'll be kind to you, and help you with the girls' luggage, Jeremiah."

"I'm the one to be helpin' with the luggage," Delia insisted.

"Be aisy." Leila lapsed purposely into brogue. "It's ourselves'll be after luggin' our own luggage up the stairs."

They were soon ascending the broad open staircase at the back of the reception hall, their happy voices blending in cheerful harmony.

Having triumphantly established Leslie in her room, the rest of the gay party went on to the room which Leila and Vera were to occupy together.

"Close the door, Beauty; and close it softly," Leila drew a long breath of sheer contentment as the four chums, who had stood shoulder to shoulder, through both adversity and joy, at Hamilton, were once more alone together. "Not that I love Leslie less, but Beauty and Jeremiah more," she added in light explanation. "Try as I may, I am not yet altogether used to Leslie Cairns as one of us. I'm glad she is, but there's still an odd strangeness about it. Who could possibly have guessed when we waged war against the San Soucians, for democracy's sake, that we should one day capture and tame their ringleader?"

"I get you. I feel about the same as you sometimes in regard to Leslie," Jerry said quickly. "How about you, Vera?"

"I like her immensely," Vera responded with a little emphatic nod. "I believe she has tried, harder than any other student who has ever enrolled at Hamilton, to conquer her faults. Leila feels the same, only she's handicapped by a certain sardonic sense of humor."

"It is the truth," Leila affirmed solemnly, then she began to smile. "I look at her as she is now, and for the life of me I cannot help remembering the dance she led us for three years about the campus. And it is at her amazing reform that I am ignoble enough, at times, to grin. Only, I shall have a care to grin over it strictly in private," she finished, her broad, humorous smile still in mischievous evidence.

"Just the same it is splendid in you to wish Leslie to be manager of the Playhouse." Marjorie spoke with admiring warmth. "Think what it will mean to her, girls." She turned to Jerry and Vera. "Her father will be so proud of her."

"And think of the hard work it will save me," Leila adroitly shunted off Marjorie's compliment.

"Don't try to slide out of your good deeds, Leila Greatheart. You're the same slippery person, when it comes to that, you always were." Marjorie made one of her funny little-girl rushes at Leila, arms widespread. She caught Leila about the neck and gave her a bear hug.

"Now I thought I had changed for the better." Leila cocked her head to one side, looking down at Marjorie with her own particular quizzical air. "But you, Beauty, I see little sign in you of the sedate dignity of a Mrs. with a newly-acquired husband, and a manor house."

"Bean is Bean," Jerry cut in, "so much the same old Beanie that I was inspired to chant a jingle to her this afternoon."

"Where then is the jingle?" Leila held out a demanding hand for a copy of it.

"Now you know perfectly well I never set down my works of genius. Apply to Marjorie for it. She got it before we both for-got it."

"I saved it for you, Leila," Marjorie assured.

"Uh-h-h." Leila received the assurance with a gratified gurgle.

"Oh, girls, it's so satisfying to see you both again, and the four of us have such a lot to talk about," Marjorie said with a happy little intake of breath, "but," she paused, her eyes unconsciously roving in the direction of Leslie's room. "It's a case of 'Remember the stranger within thy gates.'" She went on brightly. "We've plenty of time before dinner for one of our famous confabs, but it's apt to be more or less noisy. If Leslie should hear us laughing and talking, it might make her feel—well, rather out of things here. She's grown as sensitive as she used to be hard since she found herself. We must make it our special pleasure to show her we like to have her with us."

"The confab is hereby postponed, but it will keep." Leila nodded understandingly.

"We were going to shoo you two out of here, anyway," Vera mercilessly announced. "If you were to continue to hang around in here until we unpacked our bags you might see"—she put on a mysterious air,—"well, something that you're not to see, until later."

Before Marjorie could reply in kind the loud honk, honk of a motor horn came up to the four friends from the drive.

"Oh, that's Hal. He's home earlier than I had expected. I won't wait to be shooed out of here." The color had deepened charmingly in Marjorie's pink cheeks. A warm tender light had leaped into her brown eyes. "Pardon me, children. I'll see you again in a little while." She was at the door as she spoke.

An insistent repetition of the call sent her scurrying down the stairs and on to a side door of the house that opened upon the drive.

"Come here, girls, if you want to see—er—well—my ideal of perfect love." Jerry had crossed the room to one of the windows, which looked down upon the drive, and was beckoning to Leila and Vera.

Peering down, the three girls were just in time to see the meeting between the two who had once so nearly drifted apart forever, but had at the last found love in all its tender glory.

Marjorie had run down the steps of the veranda in the same instant in which Hal had sprung from the driver's seat of the roadster. They met midway on the walk, catching hold of hands, and laughing like two children. No embrace passed between them, other than the cling of hands, but there was a light upon both young faces that told its own story.

"You know whereof you speak, Jeremiah." It was Leila who lifted the brief silence that had fallen upon the three unseen watchers at the window after Hal had taken Marjorie by an arm and piloted her fondly up the steps and into the house. "There is an old Irish saying," she continued: "'Love is like a four-leaved shamrock, hard to find, but of great good luck to the finder.' And it's easy to point out the two lucky finders."

CHAPTER IV

TRUE LOVE'S OWN SYMBOL

"My dear child, I'm going to say good-bye now to Jerry Macy and take myself off downstairs so as to be ready to be among the first to say, 'Good fortune to Jerry Seabrooke'."

Miss Susanna Hamilton folded Jerry in her arms, kissing her gently upon both cheeks, and then upon her lips. The little old lady, charming in her gown of ecru satin and duchess lace, was smiling at Jerry, a world of affection in her small bright eyes.

"Dearest Goldendede." Jerry returned the embrace with fervor. "I love you bushels as Jerry Macy, and when I'm Jerry Seabrooke, I'll go on loving you, even more than bushels."

"That's worth looking forward to." Miss Susanna wagged her head with amused appreciation.

"I'm next, Jerry, dear." Mrs. Dean now claimed Jerry. "It seems hardly more than yesterday since you and Marjorie went raiding the Dean kitchen after school on a hunt for chocolate cake. Romance was far from your thoughts then. Marjorie found hers, and you yours. We are all happy in your happiness tonight." Mrs. Dean's tones bespoke her love for Jerry. "Wonderful things have befallen the Dean Army."

"I think I'm the luckiest girl in the world, Captain." Jerry brought a hand to her forehead in playful salute. "Besides Father and Mother and Hal I've you and General and Miss Susanna as special superior officers to wish me happiness. Some honor for Lieutenant Macy, I'll say."

"And you never counted me in." Marjorie shook a finger at Jerry. Seated on a chaise longue she had thus far been a contentedly-smiling, silent spectator to the fond little scene of which Jerry formed the center.

"Oh, *you're* my brother officer. I take you for granted," Jerry assured her.

It was half-past seven by the busily ticking Dresden clock on Jerry's chiffonier. At eight o'clock that evening Jerry was to be married to Danny Seabrooke in the Macy's beautiful salon-like drawing room downstairs. She had been dressed for half an hour for the momentous journey she was soon to take down the grand staircase, and on her flower-decked way to keep a high tryst with Danny, her devoted cavalier of high school days.

Mrs. Dean, Miss Susanna and Marjorie had been spending an intimate half hour with the bride-to-be in accordance to her forceful plea: "For goodness sake stick to me." The two older women now left the room to take their places among the guests. Only Marjorie remained with her chum, knowing that Jerry wished her to do so.

As the door closed upon Miss Susanna and Mrs. Dean, Jerry walked over to the long triple-plated floor mirror and began a critical survey of her resplendent self in it. Marjorie sat watching her with proud, admiring eyes. She thought she had never before seen Jerry look so pretty.

"Well, Bean," Jerry presently turned away from the mirror to fix round, inquiring blue eyes almost solemnly upon Marjorie, "what's the verdict? I mean, how does Jeremiah look?"

"You are so lovely in your wedding dress, Jerry." Marjorie gave a sigh of delighted admiration.

"Honestly, and truly *am I*—*do* I look as nice as that?" Jerry's cheeks grew pinker at the tribute.

"Honestly, and truly you are—you do," Marjorie assured with amused emphasis. "You know I've always liked best to see you wear white. But tonight—you are positively stunning, Jeremiah. Your wedding dress is a dream, and so are you in it."

"Oh, gee, but I'm glad of it," Jerry gave a sigh of profound relief. "Since it's you who is saying it, I have to believe it. I'd like to look—um-m, something celostrous, all on Danny's account. I want him to be properly impressed by my—ahem—resplendent beauty," Jerry giggled, her sense of humor ever to the fore. There was, nevertheless, something of girlish wistfulness in her joking words.

"He will be," Marjorie devotedly predicted. "What do *you* think of yourself in your wedding finery?" she continued mischievously.

"Oh, pretty fair, Bean; just middling." There was a pleased gleam in Jerry's eyes, however, as she turned once more to the mirror.

She made a charming picture standing before it, looking taller and slimmer than was her wont in the straight beautiful lines of her ivory satin wedding gown with its garniture of pearls and rare old lace. The lace-trimmed court train, falling from the shoulders, the long tight sleeves and the V-shaped pearl-embroidered neck also served to heighten the stately effect of her costume.

"I shan't put on my veil until the last minute," she announced matter-of-factly. "Just let me tell you this, Bean, it's a whole lot more trouble to dress for one's own wedding than it is for some one else's."

Mindful of her snowy finery she sat down carefully on the edge of her bed and viewed Marjorie with a half abashed, half impish air. "How's that for a sweetly sentimental thought to trot along to the altar?" she asked.

"It's strictly a la Jeremiah, only you'll forget it the instant you hear the wedding march." A reminiscent gleam had appeared in Marjorie's eyes.

"I guess you know what you are talking about." Jerry fell into sudden silence. Apparently unsentimental Jerry was not lacking in either sentiment, or emotion. She was feeling deeply the tension of the moment, but was endeavoring to hide it, even from Marjorie. "I only hope I keep in step with it," she added with a reflective air.

"In step with what?" Marjorie came suddenly out of her moment of dreaming.

"The wedding march, of course," Jerry replied with a faint chuckle.

"Oh," Marjorie had to laugh with her. She understood Jerry, and the way she was feeling, also the facetious effort her chum was making to conceal her real feelings.

"I never did like having a lot of fuss made over me." Jerry rose and walked to a side table on which reposed her wedding bouquet of lilies of the valley and white orchids. "Isn't it beautiful?" she said, lifting it up almost reverently. Her humorous expression had vanished into one of girlish seriousness.

"I love it. It's so perfect"—Marjorie paused—"as perfect as love. It's true love's own symbol."

"True love," Jerry repeated musingly. "I never dreamed for a minute when Danny and I used to squabble and play jokes on each other as high school pals that I'd ever love him enough to marry him. You know I always said I was never never going to be married." For a moment she bent her face over the mass of exquisite white blooms, hiding it from view. She presently raised it from the bouquet with: "Times have certainly changed, Beanie. They certainly have changed."

"It looks that way, Macy," Marjorie gaily agreed. Gradually her smile faded. "Jerry," she began slowly, "you know you and I have never talked much to each other about Hal—and—and—the way things were for so long between us before—well—before I discovered that I really had a heart for love. At that time I was relieved because you tried never to let me think you were disappointed because I didn't then love Hal. I felt that you were, and I often wished to have a talk with you about him. Somehow I couldn't bring myself to speak of him, even to you. I was so sure that I could never learn to love him in the beautiful way I believed he loved me. Captain was the only one I confided my troubles to."

"You weren't to blame because you didn't know your own heart," Jerry made loyal defense. "I used to feel a little out of patience with you at times. It hurt me like sixty to see Hal try to buck up, determined not to show what a crusher you had handed him. Still, I couldn't blame you, either. Love's the world's great mystery, even if it is love that sends the old ball dizzying around," Jerry finished with slangy philosophy.

In spite of her practical tone Marjorie glimpsed a glint of tenderness in her chum's eyes as she gently deposited the white armful of fragrance upon the table again.

"I've not yet forgiven myself for having hurt Hal so. Whenever I think of how nearly I lost him forever by my own blindness, it sends my heart away down for a minute. It will take a lifetime of devotion on my part to make it up to him. We're so happy together now. It doesn't seem as though I deserved such happiness," Marjorie ended half wistfully.

"Shucks," was Jerry's comforting opinion. "You deserved happiness more than any one of us did."

"Oh, no," Marjorie shook her head gravely. "No one deserves to be happier than you and Danny are going to be. You two just simply drifted beautifully into love. There haven't been any misunderstandings, or heartaches, in your romance. It's been ideal."

"That's so." Jerry considered Marjorie's assertion with a half embarrassed flush. It was the witching, intimate hour for confidences between the chums. "I guess we began to miss each other a lot at about the same time. I missed Danny dreadfully during my senior year at Hamilton. When we came to compare notes, last summer at Severn Beach, we found we weren't crazy about having to be so far away from each other and—that's the way it all happened," she confessed half shyly. "Danny wanted to ask me to marry him on that night when we went for a sail in the *Oriole* and Hal sang the 'Venetian Boat Song' with a kind of heart-break in his voice that he hadn't the least idea was there. You missed it entirely, but it got both Danny and me. I'll never forget that night as long as I live." Jerry made an eloquently reminiscent gesture. "He told me after we became engaged that he hadn't the courage to ask me that night to marry him, for fear I might turn him down as you had Hal."

"That was a night I had some very sad memories of, long afterward, when I came to a realization that I really loved Hal, but too late. I surmised he was going to ask me to marry him before I went back to Hamilton, and I was determined not to give him an opportunity. Wasn't I stony-hearted though?" Marjorie laughed rather tremulously.

"You're bravely over it now, and that's what counts," was Jerry's sturdy philosophy. "I think that when———"

"Jerry, dear, the girls will be here in a minute." Mrs. Macy's hurried entrance into the room broke up the confidential session. A plump dainty little figure in her handsome gown of pearly gray and white, her bright blue eyes adoringly took in the charming spectacle of Jerry in her brave white array. "Shall I help you with your veil?" She nodded briskly toward the beautiful, voluminous veil of brussels net which swept fairy-like folds across the foot of Jerry's bed.

"Please do, Mother." The two exchanged fond smiles.

Mrs. Macy lifted the misty, exquisite lace cloud from the bed and trotted over to Jerry with it. Jerry stood very still while her mother placed the coronet-like cap, with its garniture of pearls and orange blossoms, on her head, and adjusted it to her critical satisfaction.

The pretty service performed, Jerry placed her hands on her mother's cheeks and kissed her on the lips. "Thank you, Mother," she said. The uncontrollable impulse toward humor overcoming her she pulled a fold of the veil over her face and peered owlishly through the lace meshes at Marjorie. "It's too late for regrets," she quavered in a doleful tone. "Good night, Jerry Macy."

"Do try to behave well during the ceremony, at least, Jerry," was her mother's laughing advice as she circled about her irrepressible daughter in anxious mother-proud survey.

"I will," Jerry promised in a hollow voice that set the trio laughing. A murmur of voices outside her door, and she added encouragingly: "Here come the girls. Kindly note my exemplary behavior from now on. Jeremiah is going to step strictly into line for the great occasion."

CHAPTER V

ALL ON ACCOUNT OF JEREMIAH

"Don't hand me all the verbal bouquets. Keep a few for your own use." Surrounded by an enthusiastic bevy of bridesmaids Jerry had at last managed to make herself heard above the buzz of admiring compliments they had been hurling at her from all sides. "Talk about a rosebud garden of girls. I'll say you're it." She stood beaming her delight of the flower-like group that had invaded her room.

Jerry had had pronounced ideas of her own concerning the color scheme for her wedding. She had elected that it should be a rose wedding, since the rose was both Danny's and her favorite flower. Moreover, Danny had a preference for a certain apricot-tinted variety of rose, deep apricot in bud, but shading when open to a delicate pink. "Marvel" was the name the originator of the variety had bestowed upon the rose, and it had quickly come into fashionable popularity. Jerry, in search of an attractive color scheme for her wedding had hit upon the plan of using the dainty Marvel rose for her purpose.

She had made a careful study of the exquisite apricot-pink shading of the rose with the result that her maid of honor and six bridesmaids, now gowned in the stunning dresses she herself had designed and had made for them, bore delightful resemblance to a bouquet of "Marvels."

Lucy Warner, brimming with happiness over the unexpected privilege of serving as Jerry's maid of honor, wore a frock of deep-tinted apricot tulle over apricot silk with apricot satin slippers and stockings to match. Beneath a wreath of tiny Marvel rosebuds her small earnest features looked demurely out, giving her the semblance of the rosebud she was dressed to represent. A large bouquet of the tight-petaled buds added the final artistic touch to her costume.

Leila Harper and Leslie Cairns, as bridesmaids, wore frocks of slightly paler apricot tulle, their wreaths and bouquets of half open Marvel buds exactly matching the shade of their gowns. Helen Trent and Phyllis Moore continued further to carry out the color scheme in still paler-shaded apricot tulle, worn over silk underslips of a delicate pink. Their wreaths and bouquets were of Marvel roses, well-opened, but not full blown.

Vera Mason and Robin Page completed the color scheme in frocks of pale pink tulle with wreaths and bouquets of the full-blown Marvel roses. The two tiny flower girls, Reba and Nella Macy, kiddie cousins of Jerry's, wore bouffant frocks of chiffon, many-skirted and of the four shades of the rose in which the maid of honor and the bridesmaids' gowns had been carried out. They had long-handled, ribbon-tied baskets filled to over-flowing with half-blown and full-blown roses and wore rosebud wreaths upon their curly golden heads.

As Jerry happily took in the gorgeous human flower garden about her she could not forbear teasing Lucy a little. Fixing her eyes upon the latter with a certain ridiculous expression which always made Lucy giggle, she said: "Luciferous Warniferous, you are positively stunning. You are enchanting, imposing, arresting, resplendent—wait a minute till I think up a few more glowing terms. Oh, yes, you are celostrous, Luciferous, absolutely and undeniably celostrous—and that lets you out. Be *very very* careful of yourself this evening. Some worshipping young man may fall hard for you, and try to kidnap you."

"Oh-h, Jeremiah Macy," Lucy brandished her bouquet at Jerry, laughing, but looking half vexed. "You are—well—you are——"

"What am I?" Jerry inquired with a quizzical grin.

"The same ridiculous old tease," Lucy retorted. "When first I caught sight of you in your wedding dress, with your lovely veil, I felt positively impressed by your grandeur and dignity. Now I don't feel in the least like that about you," Lucy ended with a faint chuckle.

"Never judge by appearances, my child. A bran span new wedding dress and veil may cloak an awful disposition. Try to regard me, Luciferous, as your former friend and razzberry, Jerry, Jeremiah, Geraldine Macy, and none other. I'm going to continue to be her to the very last minute."

"The last minute is not far off, dear," Mrs. Macy now broke in. "It's a quarter to eight, children. Marjorie and I must go downstairs." She cast a covertly significant glance at Marjorie who returned it with an equally guarded flash of brown eyes. "You had best form in line, girls, as soon as we are gone so as to be ready on the dot. I'll leave the door open as we go. Remember, as soon as you hear the first notes of the wedding march you must begin to move forward to the stairs."

With these final solicitous directions Mrs. Macy went to the door and opened it wide. From below stairs the wedding party now caught the harmonious throb of violins softly entuning an old Italian wedding song. It was a marvelous old song, full of impassioned harmony, which had been one of Laurie's "finds" during his and Constance's first year abroad. Virtuoso Stevens was playing it now, accompanied by Uncle John Roland, his foster brother-musician, Charlie Stevens, and four other of the musicians who had helped to form the little orchestra, so dear to the Sanford High School boys and girls of former days. These were the musicians Jerry had chosen to make the music at her wedding.

Mrs. Macy paused for an instant in the open doorway, smiling. Her eyes roved again to the clock, now showing almost ten minutes to eight, then again to Marjorie. The latter, radiantly lovely in a sleeveless evening frock of orchid satin, a great cluster of orchids, brought her by Hal, nestling against one dimpled shoulder, stood near Jerry, head bent a trifle forward, an expression of expectant listening upon her face.

Above the overtones of the violins there suddenly arose the sweetness of a high soprano voice, taking up the ancient wedding song. A hush had already fallen upon the lately buzzing girl company with the first sound of the orchestra music. The stillness deepened as the golden voice sang on, soaring, lark-like to entrancing heights. Then Jerry shattered the spell with an exultant shout of "Connie, Connie! It's Connie singing! I know it is! Oh, you Marjorie Dean." She whirled about and pounced joyfully upon Marjorie, catching her by the shoulders and gently shaking her. "You *knew* she was coming—knew all the time, and never said a word."

"Hands off. You'll rumple your veil, and crush my orchids." Marjorie wriggled free of Jerry's lightly pinioning hands.

"I'm going to shake Mother next." Jerry made a laughing dive at her mother. "You're just as guilty as Marjorie. You knew it, too."

"We'll steal one more minute to explain, then we must run. We did not know surely till this morning that Connie and Laurie would be here to the wedding. They managed to catch a fast boat home from Havre, and arrived here only an hour ago—*all on account of Jeremiah*. We wanted you to have a last Jerry Macy surprise. Dearest pal," Marjorie's arms enfolded Jerry, regardless of her own recent admonition of "Hands off!" She kissed Jerry on the lips, saying, "You know all I wish for you," then released her and scampered for the stairs in Mrs. Macy's wake.

Silence fell again in the room with Marjorie's and Mrs. Macy's exit. Constance had begun the second verse of the song. Presently the glorious voice had ceased with a last high, dulcet note. A sighing breath of appreciation rose from the charmed listeners in Jerry's room. Still under the spell of the song and the singer, no one spoke. Then, in the midst of the stillness, the orchestra below began the Mendelssohn wedding march, very softly at first with a gradual increase of volume as the march was continued.

Came a quick scurrying into place, accompanied by soft exclamations and subdued laughter, then the bridal procession had formed and begun to move down the hall to the grand stairway.

At the foot of the broad staircase Jerry's father awaited her. On his arm she continued her little journey of love, attended by her faithful maids. Across the wide reception hall, through a ribboned aisle, which continued on into the salon, and down the middle of the long apartment to its southern end, the bridal procession swept. Its objective was a gorgeous bank of palms and roses in front of which Jerry and Danny were to make their vows. Everywhere in the salon roses were massed in fragrant profusion. The scent of the queenly flower hung over the room like sweet incense.

The clergyman who was to perform the ceremony had been the one to baptize both Jerry and Danny as infants. He had already taken his place before the rose bank. Near him Danny, accompanied by his brother, Robert, his best man, awaited the coming of the bride. Danny's serious moments of life had been thus far rare. His impish smile was more apt than not to be in evidence wherever he went. There was now no sign of it on his gravely-earnest features as he stood waiting for Jerry. Seriousness vastly became frolicksome Danny, making him handsome in spite of his freckles.

As the white-robed bride, the little girl with whom he had grown up, came toward him in her brave snowy array, the eyes of the pair met. Jerry saw the light of love leap into her bridegroom's eyes like a flashing, sacramental flame, and was blushingly content. She had at last succeeded in making "some impression" upon Danny.

CHAPTER VI

THE HIGH TRYST

The space on each side of the ribboned aisle from its beginning at the foot of the staircase to its terminus in front of the rose bank was thronged with guests. Came a subdued murmur from the friendly assemblage and a great craning of necks as the bridal cortége passed through the ribboned lane on its way to the altar.

The musicians had been stationed just inside the wide double doorway between the hall and the salon. Despite the stellar role which had been assigned to Jerry in the drama of Romance she managed to turn her head toward the orchestra, sending a fleeting, affectionate glance toward the slender golden-haired young woman smiling radiantly at her from a seat among the musicians.

Immediately the procession had passed the orchestra, Constance and Laurie rose and followed in order to join a certain small group of persons who were standing a little at the right of the altar. It comprised Mrs. Macy, Mr. and Mrs. Dean, Mr. and Mrs. Seabrooke and Jerry's Sanford married chums, together with their husbands. There was Irma Linton, now Irma Norwood, and her ever devoted cavalier of high-school days, the "Crane." Connie and Laurie, Marjorie and Hal, and Susan Atwell, now Susan Armstrong, with her tall bronzed western mate. Of the original sextette of Sanford youngsters who had been such famous pals Muriel Harding Lenox and her husband alone were missing. Jerry and Danny had been united in their desire to have near them during the ceremony those who had ever been, and would ever be, to them, their nearest, and dearest.

Followed the breathless hush which invariably precedes the momentous interval between the cessation of the wedding march and the beginning of the sacred ceremony of marriage. Followed the minister's deep, resonant enunciation of "Dearly beloved," as he took up the solemn words of the ceremony.

Marjorie alone heard Hal's "Dearest," murmured in her ear as one of his hands closed tenderly over her slim fingers. She returned the fervent pressure, a quick mist of tears blurring her eyes. Hal had put an infinity of meaning into that one murmured word of endearment, given to her alone to understand.

"My own dear wife," Danny was saying to Jerry as he kissed her with a smile which Jerry ever after fondly cherished as the most beautiful smile she had ever seen on a man's face.

A moment more, and she was receiving the congratulatory embraces of her father and mother. Next Hal kissed her, then passed her on to Marjorie. The smiling group of dear ones now hemmed the bridal pair in, eager to wish them good fortune.

Jerry and Connie met with wide-open arms, hugging each other with delighted vigor.

"You certainly put one over on me, you rascal!" Jerry exclaimed with slangy disregard for her newly-fledged title of Mrs. Daniel Seabrooke. "Oh, Connie, you can't possibly guess how glad I felt to hear your dear voice singing the wedding song! I wanted to rush downstairs, then and there, and hug you. We'd given up hoping you and Laurie might be here at the wedding, and Danny was awfully blue about it. He had counted on Hal and Laurie and the 'Crane' as his special standbys."

"I had no idea you esteemed me so highly, Dan-yell." Laurie's laughing voice broke in. He had fixed mischievous blue eyes upon Danny, face alight with the old love of teasing which had never yet failed to draw his freckled-faced pal into good-natured argument.

Danny's becomingly serious expression had now vanished in a challenging grin. He could not resist the joy of a verbal tilt with Laurie.

"You know it now, but don't let it turn your head," he cautioned. "Absence caused me to think kindly of you. Now that you are here, my future good opinion of you will depend entirely upon the way you treat me. As a bran-new, extremely well-behaved husband I am entitled to your profound respect. As yet I see no flourishing signs of it in your manner toward me. I shall hope for the best, however," he ended with mock encouragement.

"Here's hoping." Laurie showed white teeth in a broad smile.

"Matters look far from hopeful to me. Never mind, Mr. Armitage. Your wife at least respects me. Such being the case, I will overlook your decidedly disrespectful grin."

"How about the one you're sporting?" Laurie affably inquired.

"You must be seeing things." Danny whisked the smile from his face in a twinkling, gazing at Laurie with wide-eyed solemnity.

"I see marriage hasn't changed you," Laurie retorted.

"It's too early in the game to pass an opinion. A wise man would never do it," Danny made reproving reply.

Thereupon both young men burst into laughter and wrung each other's hands all over again.

"Believe me, I'm glad to have a grip on that good old hand," Danny said seriously as he gave Laurie's hand a final shake.

"Same here," Laurie made warm response.

Further friendly exchange of pertinent pleasantries between them was cut short by the congratulatory demands upon Danny's attention. Laurie and Connie also came in for a rush of cordial greeting from numerous old friends present at the wedding.

As a pretty courtesy to the guests, Reba and Nella, the little flower girls now circulated among them, giving them the roses from their baskets. There was to be a wedding supper in a huge tent that had been put up on the lawn, and also dancing in the ball room. Jerry and Danny would not leave on their wedding trip until after midnight in time to board a one-o'clock train that was to take them to the Adirondacks, where they had elected to spend their honeymoon in Hal's camp.

"I'm going to have my wedding party just like the parties Hal and I used to give," Jerry had said. "The minute the ceremony's over—good-bye formality. Danny and I have arranged to go away on a late train, purposely, so that we can stay a while with the crowd and have a dandy good time."

The first animated rush of congratulation having spent itself, Jerry and Danny separated briefly. Danny's three Sanford pals had claimed him for their own for a few merry minutes of conversation. Jerry had a mission of her own to perform in which her bridesmaids were buoyantly interested. Each was hopeful that she might be the one to catch the bridal bouquet which Jerry was presently to throw among them.

Jerry-like she was now laughingly refusing to tell her watchful attendants just when, and from what point, she intended to cast the flowery token among them.

"Follow me, and see what happens," she teased as she began a slow walk down the salon, and toward the reception hall, surrounded by a laughing, expostulating seven.

"Don't worry. You couldn't lose us if you tried," Helen Trent assured the bride.

"You ought to give Robin and me a special tip-off, Jeremiah. What chance have we against five tall, long-armed ladies?" Vera complained plaintively.

"Pay no attention to Midget," counseled Leila. "What she lacks in height she makes up in quickness. If she does not snap up the bouquet from under our very noses it will not be for lack of trying."

"It's sportsmanlike to try out this grab game, but if it means 'Leslie, you'll be married next,' then I hope I miss," Leslie confided to Leila in an undertone. "I've contracted to keep house for Peter the Great for the next few years, so that lets me out," she averred with her slow smile.

"I am fondling no hopes in that direction, either," Leila murmured. "My ideal is a nice, white-haired old gentleman who will defer to me on all occasions; one who will enjoy being unmercifully bossed." She rolled her blue eyes drolly at Leslie, who giggled softly.

"When you find him, don't forget to invite me to your wedding," she stipulated.

"You shall be my maid of honor," Leila made affable promise. "By then, we shall be old and gray, I am afraid, and be wearing bonnets and spectacles."

Jerry and her alert following had now reached the foot of the grand stairway. She set one slim, satin-shod foot upon the first step of the staircase as though about to begin the ascent of the stairs. Then she suddenly whirled about and tossed her bridal bouquet high in the air, well above the heads of the eager group of girls. A wild scramble for it ensued, accompanied by excited feminine cries. An instant, and a shout of gay laughter ascended from the animated group. Came a merry chorus of: "Leila's going to be married next. Leila's going to be married next."

CHAPTER VII

CONSPIRATORS OF HAPPINESS

"Who is he, Leila?" Helen Trent teasingly called out.

"Yes, who is he, and where did you first meet him?" Leslie Cairns, usually the most silent among the group, could not refrain from joining in the teasing.

"A fine Irish gentleman, of course," Robin said with elaborate positiveness.

"I must begin practicing old Irish airs," Phil supplemented with an energetic nod. "I may be asked to play at the wedding."

"It is valuable time you will be wasting in the practice," came in ironic tones from behind the big bouquet. The bride's flowery insignia had dropped squarely into Leila's open arms at the second when she had dashed forward with the others. Her arms still enwrapping the floral grace, she had ducked her black head until only the crown of it showed above the top of the bouquet.

"Don't pretend to be so shy! We know you aren't blushing," Vera exclaimed.

"How can you know when you can not see my face?" came pithily from behind the white shelter. Leila's face popped up above the flowers. She peered over them at her tormentors with an expression of such ludicrous shyness as to produce a gale of laughter.

"Now laugh at me," she said reprovingly, "and that after you have had a fine time making fun of me. And it's that embarrassed I am. I am all but tongue-tied from bashfulness."

"We'd never have suspected such a thing. So glad you told us." Even staid Lucy felt impelled to join in the merry badinage.

"Let me tell you more. If I am the one to be married next, then none of the rest of you will ever be married. So you may practice your Irish airs and play them to me, Phil, for my wedding day is like an Irish myth, something that will never come true."

"Such a cheerful prediction," commented Robin Page.

"Is it not?" beamed Leila.

"You really can't expect us to take you seriously, you know," Helen said with regretful scepticism.

"I expect nothing else except that you will be making me a sad lot of future trouble by teasing me on all occasions. I shall soon have no comfort at all, at all," Leila made rueful forecast.

"Never mind," Lucy lightly sympathized. "You have the bouquet. I was hoping I'd catch it, just because it is so beautiful."

"A fine bunch of posies it is," Leila lapsed into brogue, "but it's yourself that may be catching a bridegroom wan of these days, Luciferous, without the catching of the wadding bo-kay."

"*I guess not*," Lucy made vigorous protest. "Oh, there's Miss Archer." She bolted from the group with heightened color for a point across the hall where the principal of the Sanford High School stood talking with Mrs. Dean. A subdued ripple of merriment followed her escape from further teasing on Leila's part. It was privately conceded among her Hamilton chums that President Matthews' son was in love with Lucy. Whether, or not, Lucy cared for him was a matter for cogitation among them. Never by word or sign had she betrayed, even to Marjorie, anything other than an ordinary friendly interest in the young man.

"Just the same, *she blushed*," Vera said triumphantly, laughing eyes following Lucy's prompt rush across the hall.

"She'll soon be in line to blush some more. Donald Matthews is here, somewhere about, only Lucy hasn't yet happened to see him. President and Mrs. Matthews couldn't come to the wedding on account of a previous engagement at a house party. Lucy took it for granted that Donald wouldn't be here, either. I didn't tell her he was coming. She is so—well, you girls know how she is. I was afraid she'd balk at being maid of honor out of pure shyness, no matter how much she cared about it. Lucy cares about Donald. I'm almost positive she does. You see I still know something about everyone even though I'm no longer Jeremiah Macy," Jerry wound up with a droll air of wisdom.

Lucy's green eyes opened wide, when, during her chat with Miss Archer, a tall figure loomed up beside her, speaking her name with politely-concealed eagerness. She was so fully engulfed by the pleasant embarrassment of the moment that she failed to note the battery of affectionately amused eyes bent upon her from the bridal group she had so lately deserted.

"Come on, girls, let's vanish before she happens to look this way," Jerry proposed. "She nearly fell dead with surprise, as it was, when she saw her future husband. Let's not add to the shock."

The little group promptly moved on into the salon. There they became immediately separated. Jerry was quickly hemmed in by further numbers of well-wishers. Leila, Vera, Helen, Phil and Robin were warmly hailed by Sanford friends they had made while spending holiday vacations with Marjorie and Jerry.

From the midst of a knot of Sanford friends Marjorie's roving glance took in Leslie, standing at the edge of an animated group, her dark brows drawn together in a frown. "Leslie feels out of things," was her instant thought. Excusing herself to her friends she hurried over to Leslie, with intent to take her in tow.

"Oh, Bean. I'm glad to get hold of you." Leslie's frown disappeared in an expression of patent relief. "I simply had to see you about something, but I hated to butt in on you and your Sanford friends."

"What is it, Leslie?" Marjorie asked with quick concern. She was yet far from understanding Leslie's complex nature.

"I've done something, Bean, something I thought would be nice for Jerry and Mr. Seabrooke. I've got away with the first half of the stunt—and," Leslie paused, looking half abashed, "now I wonder how I'm going to get away with the last half. I thought it would be easy, but—well—I find it isn't. It's just struck me that Jerry and her husband may think I have a colossal nerve to—to——" Leslie stopped, coloring. "You'll have to help me out, Bean," she said desperately, with a short laugh.

"Of course I will. Tell me what you'd like me to do for you. I know you've planned something lovely for Jerry and Danny," encouraged Marjorie.

"Maybe." Leslie still looked doubtful. "All right. Here goes. You see since my father went to London there's no one except me to use his private car on the railroad. I knew Jerry and Mr. Seabrooke were going to the Adirondacks on their honeymoon, so I thought it would maybe please them to go there in Peter's car. If I had thought of it sooner, I'd have told Jerry about it. It never occurred to me until day before yesterday, and I've had to do some little hustling to get the car here in time. Believe me, I've kept the wires hot between here and New York. The car's here; it came in at two o'clock this afternoon, and I was right there at the station yard to welcome it. I dropped out of the gang this afternoon, but they were all so busy they didn't miss me. Now that's part one—very nice and easy. What?" Leslie's deliberate smile showed itself.

"Yes; What? You delightful plotter of happiness." Marjorie's face was alight with appreciation of Leslie's plan. "Now that you've planned the surprise, and had all the trouble to make it come true, you want me to tell them about it. No, siree; you're going to tell them about it *yourself*."

"I can't. I won't. I thought once I could, but I've got cold feet now. Please tell them, Beanie Bean. I haven't the nerve."

"You've always said you had nerve enough for anything," came Marjorie's smiling retort.

"I know it. I say a great many foolish things," Leslie admitted with a faint chuckle. "Are you going to stand by me, or are you going to quit me cold?"

"I'll help you a little," Marjorie conceded teasingly. "I'll find Jerry and Danny and steer them into the library after the company have mostly gone upstairs to the ball room. Then you are to break the news to them."

"Oh, no, I———"

"Oh, yes, you must. You haven't the least idea of what a fine surprise you are going to give Jerry. She'd like to hear it from you, Leslie. She is very fond of you."

"But she used to hate me like poison, both she and Leila Harper. I know they like me now," Leslie went on quickly. "They've shown that much. Jerry, by asking me to be one of her bridesmaids, and Leila, by asking me to be business manager of the Playhouse. I'm beginning to feel at home with Leila, but with Jerry, somehow, it seems almost as though there was a barrier still standing between us. I get it dimly that she hasn't, perhaps, ever forgiven me for the contemptible things I once tried to put over on you. I felt really pleased with myself about this car business, until I began thinking that *she* might not be pleased at all. You understand what I mean. It's hard to try to explain." Leslie fixed suddenly somber eyes upon Marjorie.

"Yes, I understand, and I also understand that you are a big goose, Leslie Adoree Cairns," Marjorie made cheering response. "Let me tell you something. Jerry would not be your friend today unless she had entirely forgiven and forgotten anything she might have once laid up against you. She would have held herself aloof from you in spite of yours and my friendship. Nothing I might have said to her in your favor would have induced her to change her mind. There; does that give you more nerve?"

"Some," Leslie brightened visibly.

"All right. Go on into the library, and wait for us. I'll bring Jerry and Danny there as soon as I can." Marjorie caught Leslie by the hands with a friendly little pressure, then sped away on her pleasant errand. At the doorway of the salon she turned to cast a reassuring smile at Leslie who stood gazing soberly after her.

Leslie's hand went up in acknowledging gesture, then she started slowly for the library which was situated on the opposite side of the house from the salon.

"Leslie would like to see you and Danny in the library," Marjorie presently murmured in Jerry's ear during a brief lull in the new tide of congratulation that was holding the bridal pair captive in the salon.

"Yours truly," Jerry returned in an undertone. "This 'wish you joy' stunt will soon be over. Tell Leslie she may expect us. Now what's on her mind?"

"Wait, and learn," Marjorie cryptically advised. Unauthorized by Leslie she gathered together Leila, Vera, Robin, Phil, Helen Trent, and, lastly, Lucy Warner, who stood talking to Donald Matthews with the serious air of a sage.

"You're needed in the library to attend a special session of the Travelers," she told each girl in turn. "Come along with me." Nor would she give out a word of information regarding the import of the special session.

Outside the library doorway she called a halt in the procession. "We'll wait here for Danny and Jerry. Keep back out of sight of Leslie. She's in the library, but I'd rather she wouldn't see you just yet."

"What is it all about? As your business partner I think I'm entitled to an explanation. Page and Dean aren't supposed to have secrets from each other," Robin made plaintive plea.

"She is that aggravating." Leila raised disapproving hands. "Wurra, wurra! What shall we do with her?"

"Pull down her curls," Vera made a playful dive at Marjorie.

"Steal her orchids." Phil made a pretended grab at the cluster of orchids nestling against Marjorie's shoulder.

"Powder her nose till it looks floury," Helen whisked a gold compact from a tiny inside pocket of her corsage and advanced upon Marjorie.

In the midst of the pretended struggle, carried on amid much subdued mirth, a calm voice inquired: "What's going on out here?" Leslie, tired of her own company, as she continued to wait in the library for Marjorie and the Seabrookes, and strolled to the door, attracted by the sound of familiar voices, gleeful with laughter. She stood surveying the group, a trace of her former quizzical aloof attitude toward the Travelers in her face and bearing.

"Now see what you've done." Marjorie merrily declared as she extricated herself from Helen's grasp. Helen, at least, had determined to carry out her part of the punishment. "You're discovered, and all because you made so much noise. Very well. You may now escort Leslie with all pomp and ceremony into the library. She has done something perfectly dear for Jerry and Danny. I took the liberty of bringing you girls here because I thought they would like you to share the surprise that's coming to them, with them."

She turned to Leslie, laying a soft little hand on the other girl's arm. "Do you mind, Leslie? We're all Travelers together you know, sworn to share each other's joys and sorrows. If you do, then———"

"No, I don't; not the least bit." Leslie was smiling now. "I thought for a minute I did; but not now. The gang will support me during the ordeal," she concluded humorously.

"Now it seems we know something of what we are about to be doing, and still not much of anything. Let us do ourselves proud as escorts, and then see what happens." Leila made a sweeping bow to Leslie, crooking an inviting arm. "Will you kindly be taking my Irish arm, Miss Cairns?" she said gallantly.

"Take mine, too," petitioned Phil, ranging herself on Leslie's other side.

"Robin and I are going to walk ahead of Leslie, backwards, into the library, bowing all the way, and chanting her praises," Vera announced grandly.

"Then I'll be advising you to watch your step, or you find your two selves sitting down very suddenly," was Leila's mirthful warning.

"We might as well bring up the rear," Marjorie told Helen and Lucy. "All the best positions have been snapped up."

Leslie had hardly more than been bowed to the big leather davenport, invited by her flamboyantly polite escorts to be seated, when Jerry's voice was heard outside the room.

"Here we are," she called out cheerily as she and Danny entered the library. Her quick glance took in the group awaiting her with a flash of surprise. Marjorie had merely said that Leslie wished to see Danny and herself in the library. "We came down the back stairs and through the kitchen so as to dodge the crowd. What's stirring?" she asked lightly, but her eyes directly sought Leslie's face.

"Nothing much." Leslie's dark eyes were bent on Jerry with smiling friendliness.

A brief instant of silence ensued. The other bridesmaids were wondering pleasantly what it was all about. Danny was showing attentive interest, though Marjorie read complete mystification on his composed features.

"Peter," Leslie began abruptly, then laughed, "I mean my father, is in London, you know. His private car on the railroad isn't doing anyone any good, just at present. I thought you two," she nodded toward the bride and groom, "might like it for your trip to the Adirondacks. I wired for it, and it's down at the railroad yard now, ready to go out with the one-o'clock train. It will be at your disposal during your honeymoon trip, if you'll accept the use of it. If you wish to go to any other place in it from the mountains, wire me at Hamilton twenty-four hours before you start, and I'll gladly make arrangements for you. Our houseman, Emil, will be aboard to make you comfortable. That's all, except that it would make both my father and me very happy to have you use it," she ended almost humbly.

"Leslie," Jerry put out both hands impulsively to Leslie who caught them in a close warm clasp. "You take my breath. What a lot of trouble you have been to just on purpose to make Danny and me happy. Isn't it perfectly celostrous, Danny?" she turned eagerly to her husband.

"It is." Danny's hand went out to Leslie. "It's a knock-down," he said, his roguish smile breaking out. "I can't think of anything to say except 'Thank you, Leslie. You've surely added tonight to our happiness.'"

"Rah, rah, rah, rah, rah, rah!

Rah, rah for Leslie and her private car!"

Phil's hands waved themselves above her head like triumphant banners as she sent up this joyful tribute. The other Travelers immediately took it up with a will. As a result more than one guest's head poked itself through the arched doorway to be as quickly withdrawn with the chagrined knowledge that the cheering going on in the library seemed to be a strictly intimate matter of rejoicing.

"It's time we were moving on, Travelers tried and true," Marjorie presently said after the hub-bub of buoyant talk and laughter had died out. "I should like to have at least one dance with the groom before these two," she smilingly indicated Danny and Jerry, "have run away from us; provided he should ask me for a dance," she added innocently.

"Will you please trot a trot with me, Mrs. Macy?" Danny grinningly rose to the occasion.

"I will; I'd love to," Marjorie came back with equal promptness. She knew Danny was feeling far more pleasantly embarrassed than appeared on the surface at Leslie's good will offer.

"If you were a bride in old Ireland you would have to dance with every man who came to your wedding," was Leila's cheering remark to Jerry as the library party started for the ball room.

"Good night! I certainly have something to be thankful for," was Jerry's emphatic opinion.

Up the familiar two flights of stairs to the ball room, a climb now doubly endeared by memory to the Sanford contingent of the light-hearted group, an evening of further jollity awaited them.

Dancing had already begun, and a fox trot was in full swing when they entered the ball room, soon to be whirled into the ever favorite amusement of the dance. Jerry and Danny had a dance together, then did not meet again until over an hour later when they led the merry van downstairs to partake of the wedding supper which would be served in the mammoth tent on the lawn.

The bridal table was a thing of beauty in the way of decorative art, and at the many smaller tables roses formed the center decoration with a rose at each place. There were favors for the feminine fair of satin-covered, rose-topped powder boxes in delicate evening shades, and for the men there were cunning Japanese rose jars filled with delightful rose pot-pourri.

The bridal table seated the bride and groom, Mr. and Mrs. Macy, Mr. and Mrs. Seabrooke and the groomsman, Robert Seabrooke, Mr. and Mrs. Dean, Hal and Marjorie, Miss Susanna Hamilton, Irma, Susan and Constance together with their husbands, the six bridesmaids, the maid of honor, and last, but not least, Delia. Jerry had ranked Delia as among her "best pals," declaring that Delia was too thoroughly a part of the Dean menage to be separated from it at the wedding supper.

It was close to midnight when the last toast to the bride and groom had been drunk down and the big tent had emptied itself of its merry assemblage, the majority of elder guests to take their leave and the younger set to return to the ball room for another hour of dancing.

"What Danny and I ought to do is to duck out the back way, cut and run," Jerry told Marjorie in the privacy of her room to which she and Marjorie had slipped away from the throng after supper, there to make ready for her wedding journey. "Make up your mind there'll be rice enough thrown at us to stop a famine in China. There'll be confetti, too. Make no mistake about that. By the time the Seabrookes dash into their car it will be hard to say which they resemble most, the tag end of a Mardi Gras parade, or a couple of rice stalks in full crop. Anyhow, we aren't going to duck. Danny and I are agreed upon that point. Nothing like giving our friends a chance at us," Jerry grinned philosophically as she slipped into the smart beige colored ensemble she had chosen as a traveling costume.

When at half-past twelve she and Danny boldly essayed their departure by way of the broad flight of steps which led down from the port cochere to the drive the rice storm set in in earnest. Amid showers of rice and confetti, and a frantic hub-bub of gay-spirited farewells, the besieged couple fled across the narrow space of stone walk, gaining the welcome shelter of their waiting car. A moment, and William, the Macy's chauffeur, had sent the trim roadster shooting forward down the drive. Jerry and Danny were started at last upon their real journey through life.

CHAPTER VIII

A "QUEER CATCH"

"And from today on we shall be driven slaves, bound by the order of good-intentioned Travelers to the ill-fare and welfare of Hamilton," Leila Harper proclaimed dramatically to Leslie Cairns as she entered Room 15 at Wayland Hall in answer to Leslie's call of "Come."

"I can stand it if you can," Leslie returned imperturbably as she gave a final pat to her smartly-coiffed head and viewed the effect with commendable satisfaction. "Thanks to a permanent wave. I'm not quite so ugly as I used to be," she told Leila with a half sardonic smile.

"Tell me nothing. I am admiring you more each time I see you," Leila spoke lightly, but there was an undercurrent of seriousness in her reply which brought a quick tinge of color to Leslie's cheeks.

"I used to think I looked better in tailored clothes and mannish coats and hats than in 'girlie' stuff." Leslie glanced down at the soft folds of the imported chiffon frock she was wearing. Silver gray, flowered with twisting sprays of scarlet poppies, with here and there a touch of scarlet satin, the dress had a peculiar individuality which was ever noticeable in Leslie's choice of clothes.

"It was Marjorie Dean who revolutionized my ideas of how to dress," she confided. "Even in the days when I couldn't even think about her without hating her, I was crazy about her clothes. They were just like her—perfectly beautiful. I took a violent fancy to one dress I saw her wear. It was a peachblow silk evening frock and I made a sketch of it and had it duplicated as nearly as I could by a New York modiste. It was just before I went home from my soph year here. I intended the dress for wear at Newport. When the dress was delivered to me, in New York, I tried it on. I looked a fright in it. I was so angry over it that I sat down and tore it to shreds and then bundled the wreck into my waste basket."

"A desperate deed," was Leila's light comment. Her keen mind flashed her an inkling of what Leslie was going to say next.

"I couldn't understand then why that peachblow dress was such a frost on me. It wasn't either the style, or the color that was unbecoming. It was the general effect of the confounded dress. It was not until long afterward, when I had come to know Marjorie, and to love her, that I found out the reason for that frock flivver. It was the combination of dress and wearer that had caught my fancy. She had given the dress its remarkable individuality. I was entirely out of harmony with her. You can understand——" Leslie paused, brows drawn in a frown.

"Yes," Leila nodded. "It would be different now, if you were to try the same thing again as an experiment."

"I couldn't do that again. You see I'm different now. I'm trying to be true to myself; to express that new self even in dress. I used to think of nothing but snatching the prettiest and best of everything that happened to please me. I was crazy to be thought very individual, and all the time my true individuality was being submerged fathoms deep beneath selfishness. That peachblow dress flivver gave me a frightful jolt, I was sore over it for weeks. But it didn't wake me up. I only wish it had," Leslie finished with a rueful shrug.

"Are you ready?" Vera's breezy entrance into the room precluded the possibility of any further confidence that Leslie might have felt an impulse to impart to Leila.

Leila had listened to Leslie's unexpected revelation with inward surprise. Leslie was inclined to be silent rather than talkative when in her company, and usually impersonal in her conversation. She broke away from her own surprised thoughts with a little start to answer Vera's question. "We are, Midget. What about the cars?"

"They're both out on the drive; I had one of the garage men drive yours over when I went to the garage for mine." Vera, daintily diminutive in a white pongee ensemble, waved a comprehensive hand in the direction of the drive. "I saw your roadster out in front, Leslie. Good work."

"Yes; I brought it from the garage early this afternoon. I've been so busy arranging, disarranging, and then re-arranging the furniture in this room that I haven't felt the wheel under my fingers for the past two days. I'm through here, at last. How do you like the lay-out?" she asked with a touch of concern.

"It's lovely." Vera glanced about her with appreciative eyes: "I adore the mulberry color scheme. Marjorie and Jerry were going to have 15 done over in fawn and blue the last year they were here. Then they went to the Arms to live, and it never happened."

"Glad you like it. I'm going to leave it as it stands when I go home to the Hedge at Christmas—as a last good-will offering to old Wayland Hall, you know," she explained whimsically.

"It's by far the grandest room in the house now," Leila said with an approving glance about her. The thick velvet rug, painted willow study table with its oval glass top, the silk-cushioned wicker chairs had all been done in a rich mulberry color. The chiffonier, dressing table and day bed were of Circassian walnut. The bed was upholstered in the same soft silk as the chairs and piled with mulberry silk cushions, corded and embroidered in dull gilt. The effect of luxurious grandeur of the rehabilitated room, however, was pleasingly lessened by the wealth of college banners and trophies, framed photographs of classmates and other treasured college souvenirs which decked the pale tan, mulberry-bordered walls.

"The Wayland Hallites will all be tumbling over one another in a wholesale rush upon Miss Remson for 15 when you are through with it," Vera made laughing prophesy.

"I shan't be here to see it," Leslie commented with a faint smile. "When I leave the Hall for the Hedge I'm going to do the Arab tent-folding stunt. Nobody except you two, Doris and Miss Remson, will be in the know. Maybe I'll will the stuff in this room to some one. Don't know. It will all depend upon what may happen. Let X, the redoubtable sign of the unknown quantity, stand for this year's college madness. Who knows the answer?" Leslie made a gesture of light futility.

"Who, indeed? I am no sooth-sayer of such mysteries, but I know this," Leila pointed significantly to Leslie's chiffonier clock, "it is twenty minutes past five, and the five-fifty train is on time. Come, let us be up, and at it." She cast a quick appraising glance in the long wall mirror near her at the smart figure in white wash satin reflected there, then walked toward the door.

Five minutes later the three cars of the self-constituted freshie-welcoming committee were eating up the few miles of smooth pike that lay between them and the railroad station of the town of Hamilton.

"Five minutes to spare, and an almost empty platform." Vera scanned the station platform the trio had just gained with a half disappointed pucker of brows. "I had hoped we'd see some of the old guard from Acasia House, or Silverton Hall."

"Too early in the game. These freshies we are here to meet are early birds. I've been wondering, whether or not, they constitute a gang; on the order of the Sans, you know. Miss Remson showed me the list of names. I noticed that ten of the addresses were New York suburban, and two Philadelphia suburban. That looks rather pally. What?"

"That is something I gave little thought to." Leila looked interested. "I saw the list, and jotted down the freshies' names, but paid small attention to the addresses. Then, too, I am not familiar with New York City as you know it, Leslie."

"Let us hope——" Vera checked herself, coloring.

"That this new aggregation won't turn out to be a second edition of the Sans," Leslie finished the sentence for her.

"Yes, that is what I half said," Vera admitted, laughing.

"Go as far as you like. You won't ruffle my feelings," Leslie assured with an air of amusement. "If history should repeat itself, it would be one on me. Now wouldn't it?"

"It's far more likely to be the other way. None of the twelve may ever have heard of one another." Vera took an optimistic view of the matter. "Hamilton has always had a large enrollment from New York City."

"We shall soon know." The long, sharp, echoing whistle of the incoming train from the East shrilled out upon the still afternoon air. Far down the track the five-fifty New York express shot into sight from around a curve.

Three pairs of alert eyes roved quickly up and down its length as it came to a final jarring stop in front of the station. The few persons issuing from the train were a signal disappointment to the welcoming delegation. No one of them could possibly be hailed as even an arriving student to Hamilton.

"Flop! Just like that!" Leslie simulated disappointed collapse. "Nary a freshie in sight, and the train's getting ready to shoot."

"Wait a minute. There's a girl coming down the train steps, away up front." Vera had spied a possible "catch." "Oh, no, it isn't," she went on half dejectedly. Second glance had revealed the traveler as a youngster of presumably thirteen, or fourteen. "She's just a little girl."

In the instant of Vera's exclamation the small figure had skipped nimbly down the last two steps of the car to the platform, laden though it was with a leather dressing-case and a good-sized black leather traveling bag.

"Upon my word! What?" broke in low, surprised tones from Leslie. "Give her another once-over, and walk out of the midget class, Vera. You have, at last, a deadly rival."

"Why, the very idea!" Vera exhibited signal amazement. "You're right, Leslie. She's not a child, and she must be at least *two inches* shorter than I."

Down the platform toward the astonished trio of post-graduates the diminutive figure of a girl was advancing at a brisk walk. Dressed in a pleated frock of bright green pongee which missed her knees by at least an inch, a close-fitting green hemp hat pulled down over her ears, she came on, confidently, surveying the three Hamilton girls with a pair of bright, jet-black eyes.

"Good afternoon," she saluted with an air of calm assurance. Her bright, bird-like eyes continued to rove from one to another of the three post-graduates. "You are upper-class students, aren't you? Awfully sweet in you to come to meet me."

"Thank you." Leila became spokesman, her face a courteous mask. "We are———"

"Seniors," interposed the little girl eagerly with a quick nod of her green-capped head.

"No." Leila's "No" was enigmatic. "We are post-graduates. We are from Way———"

"Oh, that's better still." The black-eyed girl dropped her luggage to the station platform and shot forth a small deeply-tanned hand. "Shake," she said. "Glad to meet you, I'm sure."

"Thank you." Leila tried to put friendliness into the handshake. Her canny Irish nature had already arrayed itself against the tiny freshman, and her too-assured manner. On the other hand, she could not help feeling amused by the newcomer to Hamilton College. "I am Miss Harper, of 19—. This is Miss Mason, also of 19—, and Miss Cairns of 19———"

"Why, you and Miss Mason have been graduates from college for *three whole years*, haven't you?" exclaimed the girl, her black eyes rounding in a kind of condescending surprise. "Oh, I know. You are both of the faculty. Some honor for me, to be met at the train by faculty." This, as she nodded acknowledgment of Leila's introduction, shaking hands in turn with Vera and Leslie. "Pardon me, I didn't catch your name," she said as her hand dropped away from Leslie's light clasp.

"I am Miss Cairns," Leslie returned imperturbably, "but we are not———"

"My name is Jewel Marie Ogden, and I'm entering the freshman class at Hamilton College from Warburton Prep. It's a toppo prep school not far from New York City," interrupted the girl. "You must have heard of it."

"I know Warburton." Leslie's tone was pleasantly enigmatic.

"Do you know any girls from there?" Miss Ogden asked eagerly.

"I have met a few Warburton girls."

"Tell me their names," persisted the curious freshman.

Leslie mentioned the names of three girls, New York acquaintances whom she had known in the old, more lawless days of her college career. She was relieved when her persistent questioner indifferently declared, "I've never even heard of them."

"You would hardly know any of them, as they were graduated from Warburton several years ago."

"How many years ago?"

"At least five, or six." Leslie made her answer politely evasive. She was self-vexed at having unthinkingly mentioned her former Warburton acquaintances.

"Let us help you with your bags." Leila came to Leslie's rescue. She picked up the heavier of the freshman's two leather bags.

"Oh, all right. So kind in you, I'm sure. I appreciate your interest in me. How far is it from the station to the campus?"

"Three miles. I must explain to you——" Leila began.

"Do you drive your own car?" calmly pursued Miss Ogden.

"Yes." Leila's vague sense of irritation at the inquisitive newcomer disappeared in a wild desire toward laughter. The confident assurance of this newest stranger within the gates of Hamilton challenged her ever ready sense of humor.

"We'll have to draw lots to see with which of us Miss Ogden will ride," Vera said gaily. To Miss Ogden she said: "We three drove to the station in separate cars. We expected to meet a crowd of twelve freshmen who were due to arrive here on the five-fifty express. They certainly failed to arrive." She waved a significant hand at the station platform, deserted now of persons other than themselves and two or three station employes, methodically going about their business.

"Twelve freshmen. Mm-m-m. Where were they to come from?"

"Ten of them from New York, or near New York; two from Philadelphia," Leila patiently informed.

"Let's move on." Leslie had possessed herself of the freshman's other bag. She spoke with a touch of impatience. "Too bad the freshies didn't arrive. Miss Remson will be disappointed. She——"

"Is Miss Remson the registrar?" quizzed Miss Ogden.

"No-o." Leslie could not repress a chuckle.

"Why do you laugh?" The freshman's tone was decidedly nettled.

"I beg your pardon," Leslie apologized. "If you knew Miss Remson as we do you would comprehend the joke. She is the manager of Wayland Hall, and———"

"I'm going to live at Hamilton Hall," Miss Ogden interrupted. "I gave the Hamilton bulletin a once-over, and decided that much, first thing. From the picture of it, it looked far more toppo to me than any of the other campus houses; really swagger, you know. I've brought myself up to believe in choosing the best, and that the best is none too good for me."

CHAPTER IX

THE MISSING TWELVE

A moment of breathless silence followed Jewel Marie Ogden's confident statement. Three pairs of eyes fixed themselves resolutely upon the complacent freshman. The three astonished post-graduates dared not so much as glance at one another. Leila was the first of the trio to command speech which should convey no hint of the mirthful state of her feelings.

"You have made a mistake about Hamilton Hall," she said in her direct fashion. "It is not a campus boarding house. It contains only President Matthews' and the registrar's offices, and a number of recitation rooms."

"Oh-h-h." For the first time since her arrival on the station platform the cocksure stranger exhibited signs of confusion. Chagrin swept a flood of red to her round cheeks. Instant with it, she frowned, casting a suspicious glance at Leila. "You are surely not trying to kid me, are you. It seems to me that as members of the faculty, you should——"

"We are not trying to mislead you. Hamilton's upper classmen are above such things. Furthermore, we are not members of the faculty. We——"

"But you gave me the impression you were," flashed back the black-eyed girl half crossly. "Why couldn't you have said in the first——"

"Pardon me. Permit me to finish what I had begun to say to you." The courteous dignity of Leila's tone checked the other's discourteous speech midway in utterance. "We are post-graduates, and live at Wayland Hall, one of the campus houses. We are always glad to be of service, when we may, to entering freshmen. You have evidently made a mistake regarding Hamilton Hall. Perhaps we can help you."

"Yes; I've made a stupid mistake." The freshman pettishly shrugged her slim, green-clad shoulders. She made no effort at explaining her mistake to the nonplussed trio of would-be helpers. After a tiny interval of frowning hesitation she shot at them the brisk question: "Which of the campus houses is the best; the highest price, I mean; the one with the most class to it, you know?"

"So far as general excellence is concerned the campus houses rank the same. Wayland Hall is a trifle higher-priced than the others," Leila answered levelly, fighting back her own rising desire to frown.

"Then I shall go there to live," Jewel Marie Ogden announced with a decisive wag of her head. "Since *you* live there, you can tell me all about it. I shall ask for a single, of course. I simply can't endure the thought of a roommate. I had a single at Warburton. Do you each have a single?"

"Miss Mason and Miss Harper room together. I have a single." Leslie's politely immobile features underwent a sudden purposeful tightening. She had decided to "hand the annoying freshman one" straight from the shoulder. "There are no vacancies at Wayland Hall," she said. "I should advise you to go directly to Hamilton Hall and explain your mistake to the registrar. She may be able to secure you a room, or at least half a room, in one of the other campus houses."

"I shall go to Wayland Hall first, and meet your Miss Remson. I imagine I can persuade her to make room for me there. I usually get whatever I want, when I make up my mind to go after it. It still lacks a week before the opening of college. A great many things may have happened by then." Miss Ogden's self-confidence had evidently returned with a rush.

"We are all at your service to run you up to the Hall." This time it was Leslie who fought back a frown. Never possessed of a goodly stock of patience, she was already "fed up" with Jewel Marie.

"You may take me to the campus in your car, if you will be so kind," was a gracious concession on the part of the freshie which Leslie accepted without enthusiasm.

"Pleased to be of service to you," she returned briefly.

"Suppose we hurry along, then," Vera suggested good-naturedly, "then we won't be late to dinner. Too bad to keep Miss Remson waiting while there are so few of us in the house."

"Your friends are awfully nice, but I choose to ride with you because I took a fancy to you," were the freshman's first words as Leslie presently started her roadster on the short run to the campus.

"You'd hardly say that if you knew us better," Leslie replied a trifle coolly. "Miss Harper is considered the cleverest student who ever enrolled at Hamilton, and Miss Mason is tremendously popular."

"Really? How nice. I'm sure I appreciate their interest in me." The little girl's glib reply smacked of insincerity. "Still, it was *you* who interested me most. You have an air about you. You're so awfully swagger. And your dress— pardon me for mentioning it—it looks imported. Do you send to Paris for your clothes? I suppose you have been across often. You have *so much* individuality. I was in Paris all summer. I brought back acres of lovely clothes, too. Did I guess right? Have you been abroad often?" she inquired eagerly.

"Several times. Not as often as Miss Harper has been, though." Leslie found secret satisfaction in her answer. "She comes from Ireland. Her father's estate there is one of the largest in the country."

"Ireland isn't much of a country, though," was the freshman's unimpressed opinion. "She looks quite American."

"Yes?" Leslie busied herself with her driving, vouchsafing no other reply. She was thinking that she would be better pleased to drop Miss Ogden at the Hall than she had been to meet her. She was not regretting the fact that there were no vacancies at Wayland Hall.

"Suppose I should be unable to secure a room at Wayland Hall." Jewell Marie had begun on a new tack. "In such case, I shouldn't mind rooming with you, if you would be willing to take me as a roommate."

"What?" Sheer surprise brought Leslie's pet ejaculation to her lips. She shot the car forward with a sudden jolt by way of relieving her feelings.

"Have you a large room? Is it second, or third floor; front or back?" quizzed the other girl.

"I—I—It would be impossible." Leslie's voice held finality. "I prefer to room alone. In the event that I should take a roommate, she would be a certain particular friend of mine, a senior, who also lives at the Hall. She is on her way to the U. S. now from Paris. Half of her room became vacant when her roommate left college last June, but I believe she and another senior have made arrangements to room together this year."

"I'm sorry you feel like that about it. At Warburton the girls there were crazy to room with me, but I felt then just about the way you seem to feel in regard to taking a roommate. Oh, never mind. I daresay I shall have no trouble getting into Wayland Hall," was the lofty, half piqued assertion. "Of course, I may not like the Hall. It will depend upon whether it appeals to me or not."

"The part of the country we are now passing through is called Hamilton Estates." Leslie was glad of an opportunity to change the subject. "We are coming to Hamilton Arms now. It was the home of Brooke Hamilton. He founded Hamilton College. His great-niece, Miss Susanna Hamilton, still lives at the Arms."

"Is that so? I recall seeing something about Brooke Hamilton having founded the college in the bulletin I sent for. I didn't bother myself about reading it. That sort of thing bores me dreadfully."

"Then you are likely to be bored frequently as a freshman at Hamilton." Leslie spoke with faint satire. "You will hear a great deal about Brooke

Hamilton on the campus, and see the result of his steadfast work and genius at every turn."

"I shall let it go in one ear and out the other," Miss Ogden waved a dismissing hand. "I'm not interested in the historical side of Hamilton College. It's the social side that appeals to me. I've heard there were more millionaires' daughters enrolled at Hamilton than at any other college for girls in the United States. Is that true?" The bright black eyes of the freshman fastened themselves eagerly upon Leslie.

"Really, I couldn't say. I have never stopped to think about any such thing," Leslie answered rather brusquely.

"But you must know most of the students at Hamilton," came insistently from the other girl.

"I know the majority of the students at Wayland Hall, but, with the exception of a few friends, such as Miss Harper and Miss Mason, I know little of their personal affairs, or financial circumstances. The social side of Hamilton is delightful, at the same time, it is decidedly democratic. Cleverness, and initiative, count for more at Hamilton than does money."

"That sounds awfully, well—dreadfully prissy, and pokey. 'True worth will win,' and 'Every day we are growing better, and better,' and all that sort of twaddle. One hears it generally about most colleges, though." Miss Ogden's shoulder-shrug was eloquent of her contempt of such a state of affairs as Leslie had briefly outlined to her. "I can tell in a few days whether, or not, I'm going to like Hamilton. If it doesn't appeal to me I shall pick another college."

Sight of the campus momentarily turned the self-centered strange attention from her own particular aims and ambitions. "It's a bully campus," she exclaimed with some warmth. "It has a lot of class." As the roadster sped on toward the entrance gates she continued to voice approval of the majestic stretch of green, stately Hamilton Hall, and its accompanying handsome campus houses.

Neither Leila's nor Vera's car showed on the drive leading up to Wayland Hall. Leslie guessed that they had driven to the garage, since they had preceded her on the return from the station. It therefore became her duty to escort Miss Ogden to the Hall, and there introduce her to Miss Remson. Her responsibility as one of the welcoming committee of the afternoon would then cease, she was thankfully reflecting, as she accompanied the diminutive freshman up the steps.

"Well, Leslie," greeted the brisk little manager as Leslie entered Miss Remson's office with her afternoon "catch," "you are back from the station in good season. I delayed serving dinner on account of the arriving freshmen." She rose from her desk chair and stepped forward, smiling at the new arrival in her kindly fashion.

"They never arrived, Miss Remson," Leslie said. "This is Miss Ogden, also a freshman. She came in on the five-fifty, and we promptly captured her. The freshie twelve we went down there to meet must either have missed the train, or else changed their plans. At any rate, they failed to appear. Miss Ogden would like to talk with you about securing a room at the Hall. You will pardon me, Miss Ogden, if I leave you now. I will see you again at dinner, or else, afterward." Leslie bowed to the freshman and made a quick escape from the office.

She went out on the veranda, there to await the coming of Leila and Vera from the garage. Her own car she had decided to leave parked on the drive in case she wished to go for an after-dinner spin. She dropped into one of the big porch chairs with an audible sigh of relief, mentally characterizing Jewel Marie Ogden as a "Razzberry."

"Where is she? What have you done with her?" Vera Mason's voice, low, and suspiciously near laughter, suddenly interrupted the mental analysis of the pert little freshie which Leslie was endeavoring to make.

"What?" she raised a surprised head from the hand that cupped her chin. "Where did you blow from? I never even heard you."

"Oh, we came cross-lots, and then around the corner of the house. Where is she, Leslie?" Vera repeated, eyes roving toward the opened, screened door.

"In there, having a go with Miss Remson." Leslie jerked her head toward the manager's office, the beginning of her slow smile on her lips. "I introduced her to Miss Remson, then fled."

"I should say so." Vera's small hands spread themselves in a gesture of comic hopelessness. "She's a positive curiosity. I never before met another girl quite like her. What a find she would have been for a crowd of mischievous sophs. She surely would have read of herself afterward in the grind book. I didn't dare look at either of you girls while she was talking to us." Vera dropped, laughing, into a convenient rocker.

"She was lucky to have been met by three staid, old persons like us," was Leila's humorous opinion. "I am still full of pride and vainglory at having been taken for one of the faculty. And Miss Remson has yet to hear that she was guessed to be the registrar. But for the life of me, I cannot understand why Jewel Marie, and grant me, that is some name, should have made such a ridiculous mistake about Hamilton Hall. I do not understand the girl at all, and I have often thought myself an Irish lady of some understanding."

"What I can't understand is this. As a graduate of prep school she should be thoroughly familiar with college conditions. Hamilton Hall is sufficiently described in the Hamilton bulletin so as to differentiate it from the other campus houses. I simply couldn't feel sympathetic with her when she admitted she had made a stupid mistake." Vera made honest confession. "She had been so—so—well disagreeably inquisitive and self-centered. It's not charitable to discuss her, even to you two, who saw her as I saw her, but——" Vera paused with a helpless little shrug.

"Her present manners will not carry her far at Hamilton, provided she should enroll here. I have my doubts whether she knows her own mind about it, and I have further doubts that she will be able to secure even half a room on the campus. It is a foregone conclusion that she will scorn the dormitory," Leila predicted. "What was your opinion of her, Leslie?"

"A human interrogation point," Leslie said laconically, then laughed. "Her college ideals seem to be about on a par with those of the Sans. Somehow, I felt sorry for her. If she stays at Hamilton she will gather some violent jolts. She's far from stupid, but she's a young vandal; her own worst enemy." Leslie had decided against repeating, even to Leila and Vera, the conversation which she had held with the freshman on the way to the campus. It had been in her opinion, too trivial for repetition. She had already summed up Miss Ogden in her own mind as a social climber, ill-bred, and altogether too self-assertive. She had known plenty of such girls in the old days, when she, also, had been a law unto herself. "Jewel Marie has come to the right place to learn—about herself," Leslie paused briefly, then went on. "She's awfully sure she knows herself now, but she's going to find out differently, if she sticks here at Hamilton."

"What happened to the twelve freshies, I wonder?" Leila commented irrelevantly.

"Oh, they'll probably bob up tomorrow. Let's go to dinner. I'm hungry, in spite of our bitter disappointment," Vera declared facetiously.

"Yes, we'd best beat it for the dining room. Miss Remson kept the dinner back on their account. It must be on now." Leslie rose from the porch rocker. Her gaze straying idly toward Hamilton pike she gave vent to a quick exclamation. "Look," she cried, pointing toward the pike. "Some little gas party stirring."

A long line of automobiles had appeared on the pike, coming from the direction of Hamilton Estates, moving in a slow procession past the stone wall of the campus. While Hamilton Pike was a much traveled road for motorists, the line of cars moving along in slow succession was an unusual sight.

A united exclamation ascended from the three post-graduates as the smart black roadster, leading the van, turned in at the campus gateway.

"Now what do you suppose that procession means?" Vera had clasped her small hands together in astonishment.

"Search me. The driver of the head car doesn't seem to know quite where she's bound for." Leslie had focussed her gaze upon the girl driver of the first car in the line. The latter had brought her roadster to a slow stop on the drive a few yards from the gateway, as she turned to address, over one shoulder, the solitary occupant in the tonneau of the machine. The high treble of her tones was carried to the three watchers on the veranda, though they could not understand what she was saying.

A moment's further pause, then the roadster moved forward again, arriving on the main drive at the point where it diverged into its several approaches to the campus houses. The driver of the roadster headed into the Wayland Hall drive, slowing down to a quick stop at the edge of the broad graveled space in front of the Hall.

"I've guessed the answer," Leslie said in an excited undertone. "I've counted the cars in that line. There are twelve buzz-buggies. The freshies have arrived, the missing twelve are on the job at last."

CHAPTER X

DANGER AHEAD

"This is Wayland Hall, is it not?" The driver of the head automobile had now sprung from the roadster and was advancing toward the veranda steps. She was a tall girl, gracefully slender in her smart tan motor coat, with straight, well-cut features and large flashing dark eyes. From under her small tan motor hat her hair showed jet-black and silky, contrasting sharply with the healthy pallor of her oval face. Her tone, indifferently impersonal, was such as she might have used in addressing a traffic officer, or other guardian of public service.

"Good evening. Yes, this is Wayland Hall," Vera's courteous intonation contrasted sharply with the stranger's almost imperious manner of speaking.

"Thank you." The girl in tan turned abruptly away from the steps and hurried back to the roadster. She paused at one of the tonneau doors for an instant's conversation with the, as yet unseen, occupant within the car, then went on to the next car where she paused again for a word with its driver.

"What shall we do, flee, or make a stand and greet our little freshie sisters?" Vera murmured.

"You have me there." Leila cast a comically apprehensive glance toward the line of cars, now stretching most of the way down the drive. "It is one thing to welcome a freshie at the station, but quite another to extend the hand of welcome from the veranda. And, if the other eleven should prove like this first haughty lady, with the flashing black eyes and an imperial air, there will be little need of our kind offices," Leila ended a trifle satirically.

"You got it, did you? So did I," Leslie said half grimly. "I hate to hang out on the veranda and run the risk of being classed as a mutt by this freshie legion. Somehow, I feel something like that coming our way. On the other hand, we're P. G.'s, trying to live up to Hamilton's first tradition. Let's stick it out, and see what happens."

"I'll go and tell Miss Remson they've arrived. I'll be back in a minute." Vera flitted into the house to find Miss Remson.

From the head car an elderly woman, white-haired and smartly dressed, had now emerged. Immediately she began to busy herself with a goodly quantity of luggage which she began removing, piece by piece, from the back of the car. Leslie watched her shrewdly, for a moment, then muttered to Leila,

"She's the chaperon, on the order of Gaylord, you know. Wait and see if I haven't said it."

Leila nodded. "Here they come," she said softly.

The luggage-laden occupants of the line of cars were now on the way to the veranda of the Hall led by the tall dark girl whose high animated tones could be clearly heard above the voices of her companions.

In the same moment Miss Remson came out upon the veranda with Vera, an expression of surprise in her kind blue eyes. "I never thought of them as arriving by automobile," she was saying to Vera. "A good thing I held dinner back for them."

Before Vera could make reply the first three of the luggage-burdened group of travelers had reached the veranda. The trio consisted of the tall, dark girl, the elderly woman and a very blonde stout girl wearing eye-glasses.

"Where can I find the manager of the Hall, Miss—— What is her name, Mrs. Weatherly?" The tall dark girl turned rather impatiently to her elderly companion. "Really, I have forgotten it."

"Miss Remson, I believe," supplied the gray-haired woman in a politely expressionless tone. "Don't you recall, Miss Norris, that I—"

"Where can I find Miss Remson?" The tall girl paid no heed to the half-formed question on her companion's lips. She had instead addressed herself to Leila who chanced to be sitting nearest to her.

"I am Miss Remson." The little manager stepped forward to meet the newcomers as they gained the veranda floor.

"Oh, are you? I am Miss Norris. This is Mrs. Weatherly, our chaperon. We made the trip here from New York by motor instead of by train. We would have arrived earlier except for a provoking tire blow-out on one of our machines. I hope our rooms are in readiness for us. We are really quite fagged from the trip. And, may we have dinner? Perhaps your maids might help us with our luggage."

Miss Norris deposited the two leather bags she carried upon the veranda floor. She did not offer a hand to Miss Remson, apparently not seeing the hand the manager had already half extended.

Ignoring the girl's half arrogant attitude, Miss Remson's fund of old-fashioned courtesy did not desert her. "I am glad to welcome you to Wayland Hall, Miss Norris," she said, bowing an acknowledgment of the girl's introduction to the chaperon, Mrs. Weatherly. "You will find your rooms ready; satisfactory, also I trust. Dinner has not yet been served. I had expected you by train. Dinner was therefore held back on account of your expected arrival. Miss Harper, Miss Mason and Miss Cairns, Hamilton post-graduates, drove down to the station to welcome you. They reported to me the fact of your non-arrival by train."

Miss Remson proceeded in her brisk manner to introduce Miss Norris and Mrs. Weatherly to the three P. G's. without giving the haughty freshman the opportunity of immediate answer to her own pleasant, but dignified reply.

"Pleased to meet you," Miss Norris's smiling, careless nod to each of the three P. G's. in turn was indicative of the precise amount of pleasure she derived from the meeting. Nor did she offer a hand to them. "So kind in you to go to the station. Thank you for thinking of us."

"You are welcome," Leila became spokesman, her tone formal, rather than friendly. She was not fond of being patronized. Miss Norris's glance wavered a trifle as she met the steady light of the Irish girl's blue eyes.

"Yes; it was certainly very sweet in you," she hastily amended, then turned to Miss Remson with: "We should like to see our rooms before we have dinner." She made no attempt to introduce the stout girl beside her to the three P. G's.

The bevy of freshmen behind her were paying small attention to their leader's conversation with Miss Remson. They were evidently satisfied with their leader's method of management. A low-toned buzz of conversation was going on among them, punctuated by frequent gusts of laughter.

"Come on, girls." Miss Norris waved a beckoning arm to the buzzing group at the foot of the veranda steps. With a condescending smile and nod to the three P. G's. she and her two companions followed Miss Remson into the house. Mrs. Weatherly also bowed to them, pleasantly, and with a curious expression almost of appeal on her plump features. The blonde girl showed not the slightest interest in them as she moved stolidly along beside Miss Norris.

"Isn't there a lift in the house?" was the last the trio left on the veranda heard of Miss Norris, as her voice floated back to them from the reception hall. "At Edgely Manor each campus house has—"

"Edgely Manor! Humph," Leslie's subdued ejaculation held a degree of light contempt. "So that's what it's all about. We may as well check out on this particular crowd of freshies, and be helpful to them by giving them a good letting-alone."

"Tell us about Edgely Manor, wise Leslie," begged Vera amusedly.

"Speak no word of it until we are in the dining room. Did I not hear you say you were hungry, Midget? I am that hungry myself, and that in spite of having been well snubbed," Leila had dropped into colloquial Celticism. "It's sadly hurt I should feel. Now why do I smile?" Her strong features were full of laughing amusement.

"One can't take a flock of geese seriously," Leslie answered.

"Not unless the whole flock comes hissing at once," laughed Vera as they entered the house.

"Even then they are not dangerous, if one turns on them," Leila declared contemptuously.

As the three P. G's. crossed the hall on their way to the dining room they glimpsed the last of the procession of freshmen rounding the corner at the head of the staircase.

"They came, they saw, and they're now safe in port. Why worry about them?" Leslie murmured satirically.

"I was wondering how you were going to end that time-worn quotation," was Leila's sly rejoinder.

"Well, I couldn't say 'they conquered,' for they haven't, and I had to say something," Leslie defended with a grin.

"You remind me of an Irish woman on our estate who once said very impressively to me, 'You may be knowin' Miss Leila, that a watched pot never yet set the world on fire,'" Leila chuckled.

Laughing, the trio entered the long pleasant dining room to find it occupied, thus far, by only three students. Miss Duncan, the freshman of the previous year who had passed a perfect entrance examination which had entitled her to the "Brooke Hamilton honor room" at the Hall, had returned early to college in order to tutor such students as might desire her services. Miss Ryan and Miss Keller, sophs of the previous year, had also returned to take up their junior estate at Hamilton.

"Now," Leslie began as the three friends seated themselves at their table, "I'll tell you about Edgely Manor. Described in a few words, it's a precious pet knowledge shop. It's supposedly a prep school to college, but it's really more on the order of a fashionable boarding school. The majority of the girls who enroll there are the daughters of society folks. Miss Tremaine, who is at the head of the school, is an outrageous snob. As a consequence, the Edgely Manor girls have an inflated opinion of themselves. I know this to be true, for my father picked the Manor for me as a prep school. I started in there, and managed to stand Miss Tremaine and her precious pets for two months. One Saturday afternoon I took a run into New York, and home. I'd had enough of the Manor. I balked, and wouldn't go back. Peter the Great had to find another school for me. I met Natalie Wyman at the new school, and liked her. I hadn't liked a single girl at the Manor. Nat was a frightful snob, and I developed snobbish tendencies from chumming with her. I know now that I wasn't ever a snob at heart. I was a democrat, like my father. If I hadn't been, I could never have climbed out of the pit I'd dug for myself. You girls remember the way the Sans ran things during their freshman year at Hamilton." Leslie fixed her dark eyes soberly upon Leila.

"I am not likely to forget it," Leila made honest reply. "I was strongly tempted not to come back to Hamilton the second year on that very account. It was love of Hamilton College, and all it stood for, that brought me back to it again as a soph. Then Marjorie came, Beauty set her good little feet on the campus, and you know the rest." A gleam of sentiment shone in Leila's eyes.

"Yes, I know the rest," Leila nodded slowly. "Seeing this crowd of girls today brought back memory of the Sans. In this Miss Norris I saw myself again, leading my crowd, and behaving like a villain. You know what a lot of trouble I managed to stir up, at the Hall, and on the campus. I have a hunch that history is going to repeat itself; not on the campus. The battle for democracy has been fought and won there, thanks to Marjorie and you girls who stood by her so faithfully. Here at the Hall—look out." Leslie laughed in her odd noiseless way. "Whatever starts here, I shall take a hand in. Because of the flivver I made five years ago I'm going to fight as hard for democracy this year as I once fought against it."

CHAPTER XI

THE INTRUDER

The three P. G's. were beginning their dessert when the freshman invasion upon the dining room occurred. The belated twelve, seen without motor coats and hats, were an attractive-looking lot of girls, smartly dressed to a degree. Assigned seats at table by Miss Remson, who had conducted the newcomers to the dining room, they made considerable noise in the way of talk and laughter, calling back and forth to one another across the three tables which seated them, precisely as though they might have been the only occupants of the dining room.

"What's overtaken their chaperon, I wonder?" Leslie surveyed the chattering group of diners with an enigmatic face.

"Where is Jewel Marie?" counter-questioned Vera.

"Maybe taxi-cabbing it back to Hamilton town," Leslie said ruminatively. "I left her to learn her fate from Miss Remson. She wouldn't take my word for it, that the Hall was full up to the last half room. I still feel sorry for her, somehow, thinking her over after having thankfully passed her on to Miss Remson."

Neither Mrs. Weatherly, nor Miss Ogden made an appearance in the dining room before Leila, Vera and Leslie had finished dessert.

"Want to go for a ride with me?" Leslie invited as the three went upstairs, bound for their rooms.

"We can't. We've been shamefully lazy since we came to the Hall. Neither of us are more than half unpacked. We made each other a solemn promise to do the job up brown before going bye-bye tonight," Vera said with a sigh.

"And we are persons of our word. You know just how it will be if we keep putting off unpacking. We shall be flitting gaily about, here, and there, with our friends descending hungrily upon us, and our poor possessions still in a fine muddle. 'Take time by the forelock.' So we shall firmly grab the forelock, and give it a strenuous jerk," Leila finished with energy.

"Go to it! Attaboy! Maybe I'll see you later; maybe not." Leslie left the industry-declared pair at the door of her room. The door closed, she went over to a wicker chair beside one of the windows, meditatively seating herself. She was wishing that the inquisitive little freshie she had brought to the Hall from the station had not proposed herself as a roommate to her.

"Nope I can't see it that way," she presently said aloud. "There's no reason why I should. Miss Remson would back me up in that." Her eyes roved about the luxuriously-appointed room, a gleam of pride in their dark depths. "Some room," she nodded, with a sigh of satisfaction. She smiled a little, anticipating Marjorie's friendly delight at the beauty of her "den." "I'll have a 'den-warming' next week for the Travelers," she murmured.

Thought of Marjorie, and her smile vanished gradually, leaving her rugged features darkly overcast. Marjorie, to whom she owed the change of heart which had brought her nothing except happiness, Leslie regarded as a guiding spirit. Given the same circumstances, it had now occurred to her to wonder what Marjorie would do. She thereupon began arguing with herself that even Marjorie might easily feel as she felt about giving up the comfortable privacy of a "single" to a stranger, merely because the stranger in question had set her mind upon living at Wayland Hall. Yet, in her heart, she misdoubted the strength of her own argument.

"'Remember the stranger within the gates,'" was the final pertinent fling of her mind at her as she left her room and went soberly down the stairs. She was tempted to stop in Miss Remson's office, there to inquire what had become of her freshman "catch." She went on out of the house instead, deciding to seek the manager on her return from the ride.

Leslie walked past the long line of cars, temporarily deserted by their owners, glad that she had parked her own roadster sufficiently near enough to the gates so as to escape the string of automobiles which extended within a few yards of it. Her knowledge of motor cars informed her that the cars she had passed were the latest models of the most expensive types. Her own roadster, exceptionally trim-lined, was no better than those of the freshman twelve.

She was soon speeding along Hamilton Pike, the fresh-blowing evening breeze in her face, the swift rush of the fleeing car filling her with contented exhilaration. Speeding through Hamilton Estates she glimpsed the lights of Travelers' Rest and Hamilton Arms, happy in the knowledge that she would be welcome at either of the stately homes, should she choose to stop. Carden Hedge, back among the great trees, shadowed of outline in the growing dusk, would soon be twinkling with lights. Home was not far off. Her heart beat faster at the thought. Once she had hated the very name of Hamilton. Now it was everything to her. Lost in blissful musing, the half sympathetic concern she had felt for the odd little freshman faded temporarily from her mind. Nor did it return until she had driven past the college gates on her way to the garage.

At the garage she found the proprietor, a short, stout man with a troubled expression, grumbling roundly at the strange ways of "them young ladies from the college."

"You should worry. Think of the business you're doing," Leslie humorously reminded. She had noted at first glance the cars of the twelve freshmen, arranged in a double row at the back of the roomy garage.

"I'd as lief them girls that was just here would take their cars some place else," he asserted half belligerently. "They wasn't like you, Miss Cairns, and Miss Harper and Miss Mason, and all them young ladies you go around with. I ain't no time for fussers, people that treat me 's if I was the dirt under their feet. I told one girl, straight out, 'I ain't goin' to lose no sleep, you see, if you want to take your cars t'some other garage. There's a couple more up the next street, south of the campus.'"

"Better luck tomorrow, Mr. Symes. Those girls were tired out tonight. They drove to Hamilton from New York." Leslie felt impelled to put in a good word for the absent freshmen.

"It'll take more'n a night's rest to reform that snippy bunch," was the proprietor's displeased prediction, the probable truth of which Leslie could scarcely doubt.

Returned to the Hall she poked her head in at the half-open door of the manager's office with a jesting, "No 'Busy' sign in sight. May I come in?"

"Of course you may." Miss Remson looked up smilingly from the cloth-bound, ledger-like book over which she had been poring. Leslie recognized it at a glance as the manager's "Room" book. In it she kept a register of the names of students living at the Hall, together with the numbers of the rooms and such other data as her position of manager demanded.

"I am sorry for that little Miss Ogden, Leslie," she began in low tones as Leslie sat down in a chair near her. "She seems nothing but a child, in spite of her self-assertive manner. She has set her heart upon living at Wayland Hall, and I have nothing to offer her in the way of a room. I've permitted her to use Miss Finch's and Miss Peters' room over night. Neither of them will be here until next Wednesday. She has told me that she is an orphan, and must look out for herself. She has given me as a reference Miss Sarah Arthur, Dean of Warburton Preparatory School for girls. She informed me with a ridiculous air of childish pride that she had plenty of money, could afford to take the best room at the Hall, provided she could secure it. She is nineteen, and, it seems, has no legal guardian. She was very frank with me in some respects, and decidedly secretive in others. She is really something of an enigma. I could only advise her to go to the managers of the other campus houses tomorrow and try her luck with them. It is possible she might find a vacancy in one of the other campus houses. I understand the dormitory has been completely filled. She is set against it, however. She is determined to find board on the campus."

"She applied to me on the way from the station for half of my room," Leslie said with a touch of humor. "I told her 'No.' Afterward, I wondered if it were selfish in me to refuse her. Do you think it was?" Leslie regarded Miss Remson with sudden gloomy gravity.

"No, Leslie: I do not," was Miss Remson's prompt reply. "Since you do not desire a roommate, you are under no obligation of kindness to alter your own arrangements on Miss Ogden's behalf. The Hamilton bulletin, which she admits she wrote for and received, plainly states that arrangements for rooms must be made beforehand, and by letter, by those desiring board at the campus houses. This young girl's failure to be business-like in the matter hardly calls for such a sacrifice on your part as she has asked you to make."

"She proudly informed us at the station that she expected to board at Hamilton Hall." Leslie's features lifted in a faint grin. "We had to explain matters to her. Then she said she'd made a stupid mistake, but she failed to enlighten us as to how she happened to make it. We found her more or less of a Chinese puzzle."

"She said nothing to me of having made such a mistake." Miss Remson showed half smiling surprise. "How came she to make it, I wonder?"

"Hard to say. Maybe she only gave the bulletin a once-over, then threw it away," was Leslie's half jesting theory.

"A plausible guess." Miss Remson's eyes twinkled. "Well, I have done the best I can for her, poor child. I hope she will be able to find campus accommodations. Did you see her again at dinner? I lost track of her after I had shown her to Room Fourteen. I had my hands full with that crowd of freshmen. I grew quite out of patience with Miss Norris. She ordered me about as though I were a maid. A very arrogant young woman. Her treatment of Mrs. Weatherly, the chaperon, was really insufferable."

"What became of the chaperon? I didn't see her at dinner," Leslie asked with a touch of curiosity.

"She saw her charges safely into the Hall, then telephoned for a taxicab to take her to the station. She said she wished to catch the eighty forty-five train to New York. I asked her to remain to dinner, but she declined my invitation. She complained of having a bad headache. It was hardly to be wondered. From the way her charges treated her, I judged her to be a paid chaperon."

"I think she was," Leslie nodded her conviction of the surmise. "Professional chaperons are quite the go in New York among society hounds. Papa is too busy playing the market, mamma, auntie and big sister can't leave the social whirl. Enter the long-suffering chaperon. All on account of daughter, who regards her as a tiresome necessity, and bosses her to a standstill. I know. I used to boss poor Mrs. Gaylord unmercifully. I'll say Mrs. Weatherly must have been glad to see the station taxi at the door."

"I hope you won't mind my saying it, Leslie, but these New York freshmen seem to me perilously like the Sans," the manager observed soberly. "Perhaps I formed the impression simply because they came to the Hall together in a seemingly chummy crowd. They may turn out to be of an entirely different sort. Miss Norris was the only one among them who annoyed me."

"They reminded me of the Sans in some respects," Leslie replied after a moment of reflective silence.

"Deliver me from any more such experiences as I had with the Sans." The little manager raised her hands in a prohibitive gesture.

"I will. I promise faithfully to deliver you from this freshie aggregation, if they should start any trouble." Leslie laughed, but there was a ring of resolution in her words. She rose with: "I must go upstairs and write to Peter the Great. He'll be leaving London soon for home, and I'd like him to have one more letter from me before he sails. Don't lose any sleep over the freshie invasion. Just leave it to Leila, Vera and me to keep the democracy plant growing at the Hall."

"Thank you, my dear. I shan't run out to meet calamity. Speaking of democracy reminds me of Marjorie. When did you last see her? I have been looking for a visit from her. I was so sorry I couldn't attend Jerry's wedding. I've not seen Marjorie since her return from Sanford. Tell her, when you see her again, to come over soon."

"I'm going over to Travelers' Rest tomorrow. I'll bring her back with me, if I can. She and Miss Susanna have begun re-arranging Mr. Brooke's library, and they are not yet through with the job. Good night, Miss Remson." Leslie was now at the door.

"Good night, Leslie." The manager nodded affectionately to the girl who had once been a sore trial to her.

Leslie went slowly up the stairs and down the hall toward her room, overtaken by a sudden sense of loneliness. She missed Doris Monroe. "Goldie," as Leslie liked to call Doris, was always a good pal. Too, she missed the merry camaraderie of the Sanford group of girls now scattered to the four winds. Of them, Marjorie and Lucy still remained to her, but Lucy was staying with Lillian Wenderblatt for a few days before the opening of college, and Marjorie was still deep in love's young dream. Vera and Leila had turned industrious for the evening. She wouldn't "butt in" upon them. Leslie sighed faintly as her hand closed on the knob of her door. Remembering the letter she must write, she brightened, shook off her wistful mood and opened her door with an energetic swing.

She was about to close it when the sound of a sob broke upon the dark stillness of her room. Slightly startled, her fingers found the light switch at the left of the door casing. Came a flood of light—

"What?" Leslie's favorite ejaculation fell from her lips. Inquiry, not displeasure, was in the glance she turned upon the small weeping figure, huddled on the floor beside one of the windows. Advancing toward it she said not ungently, "What's the trouble?"

CHAPTER XII

A LITTLE SOCIAL CLIMBER

The black curly head of the sobbing intruder slowly raised itself from her arms at Leslie's inquiry. The expression of the round, tear-stained face she turned toward Leslie was a mixture of shame, defiance and appeal.

"I know I've no business to be here," she quavered half apologetically. "I mean like this." Steadying her voice, she went on with: "I knocked on your door. It was open a little. When I knocked it opened wider. Then I saw there was no one in here. I thought perhaps you'd be back soon, and wouldn't mind if I waited for you. I just had to see you I feel so-o ba-d-d." The words ended in a mournful child-like wail. The girl's black curly head went down again upon her arms.

"Don't cry. Buck up, and get up," advised Leslie tersely. "Have a chair, then go ahead and spill your troubles." She already had a shrewd idea of the nature of Jewel Marie Ogden's business with her.

She waited until the downcast freshman had risen from the floor, to slump dejectedly into the depths of a broad-armed wicker chair, then she seated herself in a chair directly opposite that of the other girl.

"Now, go ahead," she directed cheerfully. "I'm listening."

"I can't find a room, or even half a room, on the campus," burst out little Miss Ogden. "Miss Remson told me to go tomorrow to see the managers of the other campus houses, but I went tonight. I couldn't bear to wait till tomorrow. I was afraid I might miss the chance of getting a room. It was no use." She shook a disconsolate head. "None of them had a single vacancy. I don't want to leave—Hamilton—I—want—to—" she faltered, her red lips again beginning to quiver.

"Why don't you try one of the boarding houses off the campus?" Leslie had decided that there was no use in reminding the downcast freshman that she alone was responsible for her present disappointment. "I know of two that are up to the campus houses in excellence. The dormitory has even better accommodations than the campus houses, but I'll say it is probably full to overflowing."

"No, no," came the positive answer, "I must be on the campus, or else go away from here. I hate the very thought of a dormitory. Nothing—I mean, not for me," the little girl hastily objected.

Leslie noted the hasty emendation with a slight smile. She suspected that slang came far easier to Miss Ogden than the "side" she had put on at the station.

"I have a reason, a very strong reason, for wishing to live on the campus," Miss Ogden began again eagerly, "I can't bear to give up hope. I came to your room to ask you if you think there'd be any chance for me with the senior you told me about. Is she surely going to take a roommate?"

"Yes I know positively, because she is my pal."

"Then why don't you and she room together?" The freshman's face brightened. "If you should, then maybe the other girl and I could—"

"No, you couldn't," Leslie interrupted patiently. "Doris Monroe, the senior I mentioned to you, is very fond of the girl she's going to room with. I like rooming alone. There; you have it." Leslie made an explanatory motion of the hand. She suspected the little girl of having designs upon her room, but of lacking the final spurt of temerity to ask outright again for a half of it.

"I guess I'd best go." Miss Ogden half rose from the chair. Then she plumped down upon it again, and began to cry. "I—wouldn't you, couldn't you—Oh, I know you'll—hate me—for being so—so—nervy, but—if you'd only take—me—as a—a—roommate for—for a while, maybe I might be able to find—another room on the campus—later. Truly, I'd try—not—to be a bother, and to—to—find another room as soon as I—could," the tearful pleader wound up with a long sobbing gurgle.

Leslie stared at her uninvited visitor, her immobile features giving no clue to her racing thoughts. She was tempted to comment with a touch of good-natured satire: "No doubt about your nerve." Immediately the impulse died, and her brain took up seriously the problem she was facing. Should she, or should she not, consider this stranger's welfare, rather than her own? A roommate would certainly not add to her happiness. Fond as she was of Doris, they got along much better in separate rooms. Her own fault. Leslie refused to blame Doris for what she was wont satirically to style as "Cairns' moods and tenses."

"You can't see me, at all, can you?" Hurt pride at length steadied the freshman's tone. She pulled herself together and rose with a kind of hopeless finality that caused Leslie a pang of self-reproach.

"No; I don't," she answered with blunt honesty, "not yet, but I'm considering you as a roommate. Don't say a word." She held up an arresting hand. "Just sit tight. Let me think things out."

"Oh-h-h I—" Miss Ogden subsided meekly, her black eyes fixed hopefully upon Leslie.

Leslie began a thoughtful survey of the room, her glance roving from one to another of its luxurious appointments. "The chaise longue will have to go. I'll give it to Miss Remson," was her mental decision. "She'll have to have a day bed like mine, and a chiffonier. I won't give up my color scheme, though I *am* giving up half my room. Good-bye to a happy life. Hard luck, Cairns II. The dress closet's large, thank goodness. I can get along with half of it. We can use the same dressing table. Hope she hasn't the mirror habit." Aloud she said: "I've considered. You may come in with me, if you like. I'll warn you, beforehand, I'm not always sociable. I like to be let alone."

"I won't bother you a bit; truly I won't. And you're sure you want—I mean, you're willing I should come?" The other girl's downcast features had lost their doleful droop.

"No; I'm not willing—yet, but I have a heart." Leslie's slow smile appeared briefly. "We'll let it go at that. I'll speak to Miss Remson tomorrow about having a couch bed brought in here, temporarily, for you." She went on to explain her plan for the re-arrangement of the room.

"I'll pay for whatever furniture you are going to buy on my account," instantly proposed the freshman. "I have lots of money. I'd love to do it."

Leslie shook her head, "No; leave that part to me. I have my own reasons for asking you to do so. Perhaps, some day, I may ask you to make me a promise on that very account."

"I'll promise now to do whatever you may ask me to do in the time to come." There was evident gratitude in the earnestly-spoken reply.

Leslie eyed the little girl with new interest. There seemed to be more to Jewel Marie that might be likable than had at first appeared on the surface. "Thank you," she said simply.

"There's something I'd like to tell you. I'd not care to have anyone else on the campus know it, though. It's about myself—a secret. No one at Warburton ever found it out—I mean—" came a pause. The freshman's black eyes were again focussed upon Leslie with solemn intensity.

Leila's jesting Celtic protest, "Tell me nothing," hovered behind Leslie's lips. She did not utter it, instead waited in silence for her visitor to continue at will.

"I believe I can trust you with my secret," the girl went on hurriedly. "It seems necessary for me to tell you. You see, you don't understand me, at all. I tried to put on airs at the station today, because—I'm not like that, really I—" Again she came to an uncertain pause. "Would you mind if I told you about myself?" She was watching Leslie rather timidly, divining the latter's unflattering lack of curiosity regarding her affairs.

"No." Leslie's "No" was kindly.

"But you are not very keen about it, are you?" persisted the freshman.

"Forget it," was the succinct advice. "Go ahead with your story."

"Well," the little girl drew a long breath, "it's like this. Until I went to Warburton prep last year, I'd always lived a different life from other girls. At the station I spoke of Warburton as though I'd started there as a freshman. I hadn't. I'd never been in any other school. I'd always had a governess. I—I'm a child of the circus."

"What?" Leslie straightened with a sudden interested jerk.

"The child of a circus," Jewel Marie repeated. "I certainly gave you a jolt that time, now didn't I?" She broke into a little laugh.

"Yes. You sound interesting. Go on," Leslie encouraged.

"Have you ever heard of 'Chiquita,' the child trapeze wonder?"

"Let me think. Have I?" Leslie considered for a moment. "No," she returned, "I haven't. I never cared much about circuses, even as a child. With what circus did you travel?"

"One called 'Fernando's Mammoth Shows.' That was a long time ago when I was six years old. I'm nineteen now. My father, Harvey Ogden, owned the show, in partnership with the ringmaster, Fernando de Castro, a Spanish Mexican. They used his name for the circus because they liked it better than Ogden for circus purposes. My mother was Spanish. She was a star trapeze performer. She and my father were married when she was seventeen."

Now started on the story she had longed to confide to Leslie the narrator spoke in short dramatic sentences. "I began working in the ring, doing acrobatic stunts when I was seven. By the time I was ten I was doing a trapeze act with my mother. We showed mostly in Mexico, and in the southern part of the U. S. When I was eleven we were caught in a flood. We were showing in a town along the Mississippi River when the flood came. It cleaned out the circus. My father was drowned. My mother was saved, but she contracted pneumonia, and died two weeks later in a hospital. Fernando and his wife, Fleurette, a bareback rider, and I were up in the town shopping when the flood came. The circus lot was near the river and a good deal lower down than the rest of the town. Twenty-two of our people, besides my father, were drowned. It was terrible."

"It must have been." Leslie had assumed her characteristic pose of elbow on chair, chin in hand. She was leaning forward a trifle, a sure indication of her sympathetic interest.

"Nandy, that's what I always called him, and Fleurette and I went to Mexico City after the flood. My father and mother had left me quite a lot of money, and Nandy had himself appointed as my guardian. It was up to Nandy and Fleurette to find another engagement, for Nandy had put most of his money into the circus, and lost it through the flood. I wanted to work, too, but none of us cared about going back again to circus life. My parents had wished me to become well-educated. Finally Nandy thought out a trapeze act for Fleurette and me. She was fine on the trapeze, too, and we went into vaudeville, with Nandy as manager. We toured the U. S. for three years, and made plenty of money, for we were headliners. After that we went to Europe and Nandy featured me as 'La Petite Oiseau.' We stayed in Europe, working, until last year. During all that time I had a tutor, an English woman, Miss Jaffrey. She was an awful frump, but she knew how to tutor. She had a sister who was teaching French at Warburton prep. She arranged for me to go to school there, without letting the dean know I was a professional. Nandy said it wouldn't do to let it be known at school that I was a trapeze performer. While I was at Warburton, Nandy took a job as manager of a vaudeville house in Paris. Fleurette grew too stout for fast trapeze work so she quit the business. Nandy fixed me up a dandy solo act and I worked, off and on, last summer at the Paris house he was managing.

"I had to carry out my father's and mother's wishes about going to college, so I wrote to half a dozen colleges for bulletins. I picked Hamilton College, but I lost the bulletin before I'd more than hardly glanced at it. If Jaffrey'd been with me she'd have written to Hamilton and arranged everything for me, but she left me when I went to Warburton. I meant to write for another bulletin, but I hate to write letters, so I let it go, thinking it would probably be as easy to get a room on the campus as it would be to get one in a hotel. I remembered something about Hamilton Hall and made the mistake of taking it for a campus house. Now you understand what an idiot I was to make such a silly mistake," the little girl ended ruefully.

"I'm understanding one thing," Leslie leaned forward, one hand extended, "you're a clever kid. You needn't be ashamed of letting it be known on the campus that you are a professional. Why keep it a secret?"

"I'd rather no one here, except you, knew it," the other girl exclaimed in quick alarm. "You must promise me you won't tell anyone what I've told you—my story in confidence. Promise me—"

"Don't worry. You may rest assured no one will ever learn it from me," Leslie interrupted. "I give you my word. There'll be no come-back."

"Thank you. I *know* I can trust you." Alarm slowly faded from the freshman's worried features. "There's no disgrace in having been a circus performer," she went on after a moment's hesitation, her tone defensive. "The trouble is this. Circus folks are mostly misunderstood by the public at large. They aren't low and ignorant as is too often supposed, the performers, I mean. They are sober, quiet, good-living people who are obliged to take the best possible care of themselves so as always to be in good physical trim for their work, which is generally dangerous. I'm not ashamed of my circus life, or of my circus friends. It's not that." She shook her black head almost vehemently. "It's only that I've said good-bye to that life. I shall never again do professional trapeze work. Entering Hamilton is the beginning of my new life. I want to be like the girls are who come from aristocratic families. I'm not. I understood that much soon after I'd entered Warburton. That was hot air, most of what I said at the station—pretending I was somebody at Warburton. I—I wasn't. I knew only a few girls—none of them belonged to the toppo social gang that ran things there."

A bright flush mantled the little girl's round cheeks as she made this confession. "I don't want to be a snob—never that, but I'd love to be what the circus crowd call 'a fine lady.' I'd love to have poise and distinction; an air, you know." She crested her black head in an unconscious imitation of her idea of aristocracy. "*You* are like that. So are those two girls who were with you at the station. The little girl was so sweet, and had such lovely manners. I'm going to try to be like her."

"Don't try to be like anyone but yourself," Leslie advised emphatically. "Make your own personality count. I don't agree with you about keeping your circus life a secret. Hamilton used to be a snob shop, but not now. Cleverness counts for more than money here. You're an artist in your line. The girls would go crazy over your trapeze stunt, and you, if they knew about you." Leslie already had a managerial eye upon the little girl for a vaudeville show she and Leila were in process of planning as a first offering at the Leila Harper Playhouse.

"No, no." There was active distress in the refusal. "It wouldn't do. Girls are queer. They might pretend to admire me here on the campus, then turn around and try to down me because I'd been with a circus."

"The upper class students wouldn't—"

"But I'm a freshman," cut in Miss Ogden, "and I want to stand well with my own class. It might make a great difference. I saw that crowd of freshmen who came to the Hall this evening. They looked awfully toppo. I shouldn't care to have them know about my circus life. I'd love to be friends with *them*. They certainly showed class."

A great light suddenly burst upon Leslie. So that was the way things were with Jewel Marie. There was nothing she felt privileged to offer in the way of advice that the socially-ambitious freshman might care to hear. She would have to discover for herself that all was not gold that glittered.

CHAPTER XIII

PLANNING POPULARITY

"The freshman frolic is to be given next Saturday evening in the gym. Miss Ferguson has invited me to go. I understood her to say that her roommate, Miss Waters, was going to invite you. Have you seen her?" Stephanie Norris's voice betrayed no sign of pleasant interest in the information she had just delivered to her stout roommate, Laura Fisher. Laura, deep in a novel, had not glanced up from it at her chum's entrance into the room.

"Nope." Laura did not raise her eyes from her book.

"Anything but a manless dance." Stephanie shrugged disdainfully as she walked to the dressing table mirror and began a critical survey of the attractive reflection it threw back to her. Tall, and charmingly slender, the violet-gray of her tailored cloth frock strikingly emphasized the black of hair and eyes and the clear, lovely pallor of skin.

"You haven't heard a word I've been saying," Stephanie turned petulantly away from the mirror to frown at Laura.

"Um-m-m," Laura went on reading.

"Will you please stop behaving like a dummy, and listen to me?" Stephanie's black eyes had begun to flash ominously.

"Um-m-m," Laura's pale blue eyes lifted themselves slowly from her book. Reaching a hand into a conveniently-near box of nut chocolates she carefully selected one, bit into it enjoyingly, then drawled, "I'm listening."

"Did you hear anything I said?" Stephanie demanded crossly.

"Not much. You say such a lot, Steve, it's hard to keep track of your remarks. I heard you say something about the freshman frolic, and then something more—about a dummy," Laura paused, a glint of malice in her pale eyes.

"You are—"

"I'm really listening this time," Laura interrupted sweetly.

"You are going to be invited to the frolic by Miss Waters." Stephanie had intended to tell Laura that she was detestable. Policy warned her to more impersonal speech. "Miss Ferguson has invited me."

"You don't seem to be crazy over the honor," Laura fished for another chocolate.

"I'm not," Stephanie declared pettishly. "Miss Ferguson is all right. I like her better than I like the rest of this Wayland Hall crowd. Hamilton is, and has been from the first, a disappointment to me. But then—I never wanted to come here." She sank into a chair, frowning moodily.

"You didn't?" Laura at last showed indication of interest. "Then why in Pete's name did you make the gang think it was the only college on the map?"

"Because—" Stephanie flushed, "I wanted the gang with me," she said lamely.

"We'd have gone with you to Smith, or Bryn Mawr—to any of the others you might have picked. None of us were crazy about Hamilton. We'd heard of it as a stiff-necked proposition, all tied up with Brooke Hamilton traditions. You said it led the rest socially; that it was a college of millionaires' daughters," she finished accusingly.

"That's true; about the millionaires' daughters," Stephanie defended. "My father heard that the wealthiest men in the U. S. favor Hamilton as a college for their daughters. He was determined I should enroll at Hamilton; not because of that. He had another reason for wishing me to come here; a stronger one."

"What was it?" Laura was eyeing Stephanie speculatively.

"I don't know," Stephanie confessed. "He didn't say he had, but—I understand my father, when he's set his mind upon some certain thing. He talked to me very seriously about Hamilton. He wants me to make a notable record for myself here; win honors, you know, and make my influence felt on the campus. He's promised me a diamond necklace next June if I succeed in carrying out his ideas on the subject." Stephanie's lowering features cleared themselves for the moment.

"Go to it." There was a hint of indolent satire in the stout girl's tone. "What are you going to do to start the noble influence ball to rolling?"

"How should I know?" Stephanie countered irritably. "The very idea of it makes me weary. I want the necklace. I know that much. I'll have to study the situation, and then try to hit the high spots at the psychological moment."

"It sounds easy. I wonder—" Laura made a tantalizing pause.

"Don't make fun of me," Stephanie turned upon her roommate with sudden fierceness of tone. "It's—it's outrageous in Father to expect any such thing of me, necklace or no necklace. I like to do as I please, without having to watch my step all the time. I'll have to see to it that I make brilliant recitations. That means digging, when I'm longing to be out in my car. I'll have to make myself popular with the girls that count as powers on the campus. That will be a frightfully tiresome task. I'm going to entertain a good deal. Father has doubled my allowance. I shall pick the best sorority, and try to make it, and go in for dramatics and sports."

"Good-bye, in case I shouldn't see you again," Laura crunched a chocolate almond, smiling at Stephanie out of half-closed eyes. "You're going to be *so* busy."

"Oh, stop trying to be funny. You can help me a lot if you choose. You can keep the rest of our gang in line to help me, too. Only they mustn't be let into the real reason why. It wouldn't do. I can trust you. I'm not so sure of the others. Through one, or another of them, my plan would leak out on the campus, and make not only myself, but my father, too, seem ridiculous. You are so clever. You can pick up bits of campus news from the students without them suspecting they are being pumped. Then I'll know exactly how I stand at all times, and can act accordingly. You'll be something on the order of a prime minister to me." Stephanie had now become flatteringly appealing.

"Yes, I can wind the girls around my finger," Laura conceded confidently. "Only they never suspect they're being wound. You get the credit as leader, while I do the managing. You're in luck, Steve, to have me around. Do you get that?"

"Oh, I know it." Stephanie had changed to sweetly grateful. Laura's boast, made in significant assurance, called for sugar on her part. "You're quite wonderful, dear," she continued purringly. "What do you think we ought to do first?"

"Get on the good side of those three high and mighty P. G.'s," Laura made instant reply. "I've been finding out a few things on the campus about them. We made a mistake the day we came to the Hall in snubbing them when they tried to be friendly."

"I didn't care to be patronized by them," Stephanie cut in coldly.

"They weren't trying to patronize us. I told you so then, didn't I?"

"Yes, but I—"

"You wouldn't believe that I knew what I was talking about. And the moral to that, my dear, is—they've given us a fine letting-alone ever since."

"Oh, I don't know." Sheer stubbornness prompted Stephanie to contest her chum's triumphant statement. "I imagine it's only because they've been busy with their own affairs that we've seen so little of them. Half the time they're away from meals. We've merely kept to ourselves which is—"

"Another mistake we've made," Laura supplemented with curt conviction. "It has cut us off from finding out things about them, and also about this confoundedly high-brow institution of learning."

"Rubbish. I've heard too much about it already."

"And about *them*?" Laura persisted coolly.

"Well; I've asked Miss Ferguson about them. She has no time for them, though she is too well-bred to say it outright. When I spoke to her about the station business, and about having met them she said in the sweetest way that she hardly knew them, and would prefer not to discuss them."

"Naturally; don't doubt it," Laura commented with lazy sarcasm.

"What do you mean?" Stephanie questioned in a sharp tone.

"Just what I say. She has good reason for pretending to mind her own business. I happen to know *that* much about her."

"What do you mean?" Stephanie repeated, eyeing her roommate narrowly.

"Oh, I heard a few little things about Miss Ferguson the other day. For one thing, she is a trouble-maker. She tried to start trouble, it seems, last year at the Hall for Miss Cairns. I don't know why. I'm going to find out, though. Anyway, she didn't get away with it. Miss Remson, and a crowd of P. G.'s who were at the Hall then, and who belonged to the same sorority as Miss Cairns, stood by her. At the last, almost all of Miss Ferguson's pals, who had backed her, turned against her. This P. G., Marjorie Dean something or other, who, according to report is the Great I Am here at Hamilton, was on Miss Cairns' side, too. Miss Ferguson didn't have a look-in."

"I don't believe any such tale," Stephanie said contemptuously. "Who told it to you?" she asked with displeased curiosity.

"Nothing doing. I promised not to tell what I've just told you, or from whom I heard it. I've partly broken my word already by repeating it to you. I thought you ought to know about it, but it's not necessary for you to know who said it," Laura answered coolly.

"No one except an enemy of Miss Ferguson's would say such mean things about her; that she was a trouble-maker, and that she hadn't a look-in," was Stephanie's scornful opinion.

"Then I must be the enemy," Laura laughed softly. "What's the matter with you, Steve? But, no; it's not your fault. I didn't make myself clear. The person who told me about Miss Ferguson wasn't trying to down her. She simply told me a little about the trouble last year, and I drew my own conclusions about

Miss Ferguson. You'll find out, sooner or later, that they're correct. Look out for her. Remember, I've warned you."

"I don't need your warning. I consider myself capable of judging character. I like Miss Ferguson." Stephanie's chin tilted itself to a defiant angle.

"Which goes to show what a punk judge of character you are," was the dry retort. "Never mind. Let it go at that. No use in raving at me, Steve. The person who told me is a friend of Miss Ferguson's, but she has a wholesome respect for Miss Cairns, and her P. G. supporters. That's why I couldn't glean much from her. Better success next time," Laura predicted, indolently confident.

"You're altogether too mysterious. You know more about—well, about this story than you've told me," Stephanie coldly accused.

"No; I don't; and that's flat. When I *do* find out more, you'll be the first to hear it." There was finality in the lightly-given promise.

Stephanie frowningly accepted defeat. She could not well afford to quarrel with Laura. Once thoroughly angered, Laura was apt to turn stonily silent, refusing to speak to her for weeks. "What shall you wear to the freshman dance?" She changed the dangerous subject half sulkily.

"Haven't decided yet." A glint of amusement appeared, and as quickly disappeared in Laura's eyes. "The pale blue georgette with the silver lace tunic, maybe. It's my prettiest frock."

"I shall wear my white satin dress; the imported one, you know. It's a stunning thing; too stunning to be wasted on a girl hop, but first impressions count. There's to be a beauty contest. How I'd *love* to win it. Miss Ferguson says there are to be no juniors or seniors at the frolic this year. The sophomore class is a little larger than the freshie class, so the juniors and seniors won't be needed as escorts. I haven't seen any startling beauties yet among either the freshies or the sophs. Have you?" Stephanie's question betrayed ill-suppressed eagerness.

"I've seen three or four beautiful girls on the campus. They may be upper class girls, for all I know. Of course, Miss Monroe, here at the Hall, is a beauty, but she's a senior, and that lets her out. I heard she'd won it two successive years. I heard, too, that this Marjorie Dean, I can't remember her married name, had won it, twice; that she was prettier than Miss Monroe, though of a different type of beauty."

"Do you think there is a chance that I might win the contest?" Stephanie could not resist asking the question.

"Yes; I think there is," Laura returned speculatively, "particularly if you should wear the white satin dress. You *are* beautiful, Steve, but—" Laura paused, shaking her head.

"But what?" Stephanie demanded, half affronted.

"You're too imperious in manner. It somehow shows itself in your face, and lessens your good points. You ought to be more gracious of manner. You'd make a better impression all around. Just try it out for the rest of the week and go to the frolic looking radiant, whether you feel like being gracious, or not," was Laura's calmly pertinent advice.

"What do you expect me to do? Go about the campus grinning like a Chessy cat?" came the nettled retort.

"It will do more for you in the way of popularity than your empress of the world pose. You asked me for my opinion. You now have it. I'm going for a ride, and a stop at Baretti's on the way back to dinner." Laura rose with the deliberate slowness which characterized her every movement. "You'd better come along."

"No; I have letters to write," Stephanie replied curtly. She was still piqued at Laura's scarcely flattering criticism.

"Then you'd better put a 'Busy' sign on the door. Miss Ogden has been here twice to see you while you were out."

"Oh, that tiresome little upstart!" Stephanie's face darkened. "I can't endure her."

"She seems to have a crush on you."

"She'll have to get over it, then, for I *can't endure her*. She's underbred." Stephanie's red upper lip lifted itself scornfully.

"She's a freshie, though. Don't forget that," Laura reminded. "Class election's next week. Be nice to her, and she may nominate you for president. Antagonize her, and she may do you a lot of damage among the freshies. Those black eyes of hers can shoot danger signals. Try snubbing her once, and then—look out."

"You're positively maddening today," Stephanie exclaimed in angry vexation. "You've done nothing but criticize me ever since I came into the room."

"At least I've said what I had to say to your face." Laura's unconcern at her roommate's displeasure was apparent. "You'd like it a good deal less if I had said it to one of the other girls, and behind your back."

Stephanie accepted the truth of Laura's calm statement with a pettish little shrug. "I shall not put up a 'Busy' sign, nor answer the door if she should knock," she declared perversely.

"It's up to you." It was Laura's turn to shrug. "Don't forget, though, that Miss Ogden rooms with Miss Cairns, and Miss Cairns is one of the high powers on the campus, as nearly as I can judge. She's a pal of the Great I Am."

"I fail to see any special reason why all that nonsense should be of interest to me." Stephanie chose to continue to be perverse.

"Think it over. So long. Shall I hang out the 'Busy' sign?"

"*No*," Stephanie all but shouted the reply.

"All right. Have your own way about it, and be sorry afterward." With this prophetic warning, Laura went out the door, laughing softly, leaving her stubborn roommate to digest the unwelcome prediction as best she might.

CHAPTER XIV

MARJORIE FINDS THE LOST NOTE BOOK

"Only one more case to do, then this job will be finished, and finished as it should be." Miss Susanna Hamilton, looking tinier than usual in the enveloping folds of a blue and white pinafore, gave a long, satisfied sigh as she viewed the completed work which had engaged Marjorie, Jonas and herself for several days.

"It truly does look fine," Marjorie echoed the sigh. Standing beside Miss Susanna in the middle of the large library at the Arms, she was a charming study of work in her pale blue smock and dust cap. "Only to think; we are the first to re-arrange Mr. Brooke's books since he himself used them," she added meditatively.

"Yes," Miss Susanna nodded rather absently. Her thoughts, as well as Marjorie's, were turning to the long-passed master of the Arms whose influence still pervaded the stately old house like a living presence.

"Goodness knows the library needed a going-over," Miss Hamilton said with a sudden change to practicality. "Jonas has kept the books dusted, of course; but that's all. I knew Uncle Brooke's books were sadly out of place. I used to help him take care of his library. Somehow, after his death, I hadn't a heart for this straightening job. Toward the last of his life he spent a great deal of time in the library. He was inclined to forgetfulness at times, which accounts for his books being so sadly out of place. They're in order again at last, thanks to you, Marjorie." Her keen dark eyes wandered contentedly from one tall-glassed bookcase to another.

"It's not yet eleven. I think we'd have time to do that last case before luncheon, don't you?" Marjorie was appraising the contents of a smaller teak-wood bookcase that stood by itself against the east wall of the library. Three sides of the library were book-lined, but the east side showed no bookcases other than the one she had just indicated.

"Yes; I think so, too. That case holds Uncle Brooke's most treasured books." Miss Susanna stood regarding it retrospectively. "Not books which might be considered very valuable from a money standpoint," she explained. "It holds the books that were dear to him, for one reason or another. He never followed any particular arrangement in the matter of that case. I daresay half of them are standing upside-down on the shelves. I left it until last, purposely. The case is locked, but here's the key."

The old lady brought a small brass key from the depths of her pinafore pocket. She trotted across the room to the case and fitted the key to the lock. Marjorie followed her, standing interestedly beside her as she swung open the double glassed doors. More than once, during her stay at Hamilton Arms, while compiling the Brooke Hamilton biography, she had wondered idly about this particular case. Its glass doors had inside curtains of a thin, silky Oriental material which lent to the case an oddly mysterious air. Miss Susanna had never spoken of it to her, and Marjorie had delicately forborne making any inquiry to Miss Hamilton concerning it.

"It's just as he left it." Miss Susanna's brisk tones had softened. She and Marjorie were gazing into the interior of the now open bookcase at the orderly disorder of the overcrowded shelves. There were books, thick and thin, large and small, even to tininess, leather and cloth bindings, standing in uneven rows upon the dusty shelves. On top of the rows were yet more books, in little piles of twos and threes, a true sign of an ardent book lover.

"We'll have to take them out, four or five at a time, dust them and the space on the shelf that they occupy, then put them back exactly as we found them," was Marjorie's plan of action. "Wait a minute, I'll bring you a chair, Goldendede. You shall sit beside me, and direct this enterprise. Let me do the work. The case is hardly large enough for us both to work on at the same time."

She was hurrying across the library before she had finished speaking for Miss Susanna's favorite chair. "There, my dear Goldendede, pray you be seated," she invited, with a low bow, setting the chair beside Miss Hamilton, "while your faithful servitor proceeds to work magic."

"I'll take you at your word, child. I'm really a little tired. I haven't your young strength, and we have delved most industriously this morning." The old lady sat down in the chair with grateful alacrity.

Very carefully Marjorie began the task. She started at the left end of the top shelf of the case, gently pulling out the well-worn bindings with reverent fingers. Brooke Hamilton had ranged literature in search of the best was her thought as she continued to explore his treasures.

"You are welcome to the key to the case at any time, Marjorie," Miss Susanna's bright, bird-like eyes had not missed the warm, interested light upon Marjorie's lovely features as her willing hands moved among the dusty bindings, restoring them once more to something of their original pristine brightness.

"How dear in you, Goldendede. I was just wishing that I might go browsing among these books." Marjorie's childlike delight at the unexpected concession was the old lady's pleasure. "This bookcase seems a little library in itself, representative of Mr. Brooke and his broad-mindedness."

"It is just that. Uncle Brooke's books were his best friends. They were dear to him because of the particular message each had for him." The mistress of the Arms dropped into one of her not infrequent intervals of silence which Marjorie had early come to know and respect. She continued with her work, content to let the little old lady shatter it at will.

"What is the latest news from the campus, child?" Miss Susanna came suddenly out of her brief spell of silent abstraction. "'I have nerve,' as Jerry would say, to ask you that, since I've been the means of keeping you away from it for the past week."

"Then, further to quote Jerry, 'I like your nerve,'" Marjorie replied laughingly. "I've loved to be here. Not that I love the campus less, but Goldendede more. I'm going over to Wayland Hall tomorrow evening to see the girls. Hal has a business appointment in the town of Hamilton. I haven't the least idea of what it's all about. He's been very mysterious over it. He's going to stop for me on his way home."

"A business appointment! That sounds interesting." Miss Susanna exhibited affectionate curiosity. Hal's one cross since he and Marjorie had taken up their residence at Hamilton Estates had been his inability to decide upon some definite plan of business occupation. Possessed of a comparatively large fortune, inherited from his grandfather, his youthful energy rebelled against settling down at Travelers' Rest as a country gentleman. Marjorie had found her work at Hamilton College, the work which had all but parted them forever. Hal hoped that he might also find a work in their new home, satisfying to heart and brain. Only lately an idea had come to him as the result of a prospecting tour about the staid, self-centered town of Hamilton. Pursuant of his idea he had got into action. The result had been his appointment with John Saxe, the real estate agent who had formerly figured in the business ventures of the steady little firm of "Page & Dean." The outcome of his appointment with Mr. Saxe would, he fondly hoped, furnish a happy surprise for Marjorie.

"Of course it sounds interesting. That's precisely what I said to Hal when he mentioned the appointment to me. He laughed, but wouldn't volunteer any further information. I didn't ask for any, either. He has some sort of delightful surprise in store for me. I know he has," was Marjorie's smilingly confident assertion.

Miss Susanna nodded smiling content of the happiness of the two young people upon whom her affections were so firmly centered.

"There's the bell." She suddenly held up a hand in a listening attitude. "Now *who* can that be? Not callers, I hope. If it should be, I shall receive them just as I am; pinafore, dusty hands, and all."

"It's Miss Leslie, Miss Susanna." Jonas had appeared in the open doorway of the library.

"Oh! What a relief! Ask her to come in here, Jonas." Miss Hamilton had bobbed up from the chair at sound of the bell. She dropped into it again, with a thankful sigh.

"Where have you been keeping yourself, Leslie?" Sight of Leslie Cairns in the doorway, looking her best in a smart ecru ensemble and ultra-trim little felt hat, brought Miss Susanna to her feet again, and hurrying across the room to greet her welcome caller.

"Yes! where have you been, elusive person?" Marjorie hastily shoved a book, held in her right hand, back into place on a shelf and came forward, dust cloth cheerfully waving a greeting to the visitor. "Twice I've 'phoned you. 'Out' was the answer Annie gave me both times. Then I wrote you a note, demanding your presence at Travelers' Inn at dinner tomorrow evening. I 'phoned Leila, asking her and Vera to come, too. They can't come because the Bertramites are entertaining them at Baretti's. They'll be back at the Hall, though, by seven-thirty, for the Bertramites have to study. Leila said, why not foregather in Vera's and her room for the evening. Now you see what it's all about. My note to you was a sketchy scrawl. I wrote it in a hurry. Perhaps you haven't received it yet." Marjorie glanced inquiringly at Leslie.

"Yes; I received it in the morning mail. I was anxious to see you, and Miss Susanna, so I took a run over here instead of telephoning. I had an idea you were still busy with the library job. It looks great." Leslie's eyes roved approvingly over the beautiful old room with its wealth of books from many lands.

"This is the last case, and I have only two more shelves to do. Please tell Leslie about it, Goldendede, while I work very hard to finish it." Marjorie energetically resumed work, making herself a mental promise to spend a day soon in the library in a leisurely exploration of the treasures of the quaint old bookcase.

Presently coming to the bottom shelf, she sat down upon the thick velvet rug, reaching mechanically for the first book at the left end of the shelf. It was, she saw, a copy of the dissertations of Epictitus, bound in green morocco, the soft fine leather worn by constant use. She smiled. Epictitus had been Brooke Hamilton's favorite philosopher, so Miss Susanna had told her. She wiped away the dust very gently from the priceless volume, then opened it, about to give the yellowed leaves a mild shake.

To her surprise a considerably smaller, black, cloth-bound book dropped from among the leaves of the Epictitus into her lap. It was a thin little book, not more than six inches long and three inches wide. About an inch from the top of the cover a white label had been pasted that bore the writing of the departed master of the Arms. "Brooke Hamilton," she read, "Personal Notes."

Marjorie's heart began a sudden joyful throbbing. Could the little black book be the particular, important notebook of which Miss Susanna had regretfully spoken as lost at the time when she had turned over to Marjorie the material for her distinguished great-uncle's biography?

With a joyful little cry Marjorie was on her feet, and holding out the little black book to Miss Hamilton.

"What wonderful thing have you found in the old case, child?" Miss Susanna interrupted her conversation with Leslie to peer tolerantly through her glasses at Marjorie.

"Look at it, Goldendede," Marjorie excitedly thrust the notebook into the old lady's hands. "It's a notebook. Mr. Brooke's own notebook; the one that you thought was lost. I'm sure of it."

CHAPTER XV

BROOKE HAMILTON'S STAUNCHEST ADVOCATE

"I believe you are right, Marjorie." Miss Susanna's hands were trembling slightly as she opened the notebook and read aloud the first entry. "'Thought of a new motto today. "Her ways led upward to the stars." Note: This motto should be particularly applicable to the "one" whom I hope may rise, a future guiding light to Hamilton College.'"

"Why—why—that's my motto." Marjorie was looking her utter amazement. "I mean—" Sudden confusion deepened the pink in her cheeks to rose. "It's the one you selected for me for citation, Goldendede," she added in embarrassed explanation.

"It's the one that suited you best, so don't feel backward about coming forward and saying so," Leslie assured with her slow smile.

"Of course it suited her," chimed in Miss Susanna. "You know, Leslie, I've always said that Marjorie typified Uncle Brooke's ideal of girlhood."

"Wouldn't you like to read us some more notes, Goldendede?" Marjorie asked persuasively.

"And thus take the subject off your very retiring self," the old lady supplemented pithily. "Very good, my dear." Miss Hamilton turned the first leaf and read out to her two avid listeners, "'Must have Jenkins retake my foot measurements. Last pair of boots he made me are a fraction too narrow. Don't forget to do this. Important.'"

A ripple of laughter greeted this entry.

"From the sublime to the vexatious problems of everyday life," commented Miss Susanna. She continued to read aloud the annotations of her famous kinsman. Short, and to the point, they revealed clearly the character of Brooke Hamilton—philosopher, sage, philanthropist, and lastly, unassuming country gentleman.

"This must be the book Uncle Brooke lost not more than a year before his death. He was greatly annoyed by the loss, and used to hunt for it by the hour. Many of the annotations contained dates which he could not remember, offhand. And to think that it's been tucked away all these years in the Epictitus! Strange he didn't find it again soon after he had lost it." Miss Hamilton knitted thoughtful brows. "Ah, now I recall something that may have been the very reason he didn't. A friend gave him a very fine copy of

Epictitus on his birthday. He placed the new copy on his desk, in his study. It was in a much larger print than the other, and his eyes had begun to fail him considerably then."

Miss Susanna turned leaf upon leaf of the notebook, reading aloud to her interested audience of two as she turned them. "There, I knew I was right about that." She looked up triumphantly from the book, then read, "'Have decided to offer the fifty-thousand conditional gift to Hamilton through the medium of "the one who may arise" in my college. I shall ask Norris to handle the matter for me. I can rely upon him for integrity, and at the same time be of financial service to him since he is hard put at present in his law business. I shall go to his office to talk things over with him tomorrow.'"

"This little book is a precious find to me, girls." Miss Hamilton's hands were trembling with the excitement of what she had just read. "Uncle Brooke had sometimes spoken vaguely to me of some such plan he had in mind for the college, but I never knew whether, or no, he had put it into execution. This annotation tells me that he must have done so. Once he had put his hand to the plow, he never turned back."

The abstracted light in the old lady's eyes spelled her absorbed listeners to silence. They continued to watch her as she turned the next leaf, waiting to hear more from her at will. The time-yellowed leaves of the note book continued to turn under her small fingers. She was evidently in search of further data concerning her kinsman's avowed project.

"Ah; here it is!" she exclaimed. "'Saw Norris last Tuesday. Have completed arrangements with him for the "Brooke Hamilton Honor Fund." For particulars and necessary accompanying papers, see secret drawer.'"

"The secret drawer!" Marjorie cried. "It is in Mr. Brooke's study desk, isn't it? Didn't you say once to me that there was a secret drawer in the desk?"

"Yes," An oddly puzzled frown had sprung between Miss Hamilton's brows. "I don't understand what Uncle Brooke meant. There is nothing in the secret drawer in his study desk. I know that positively because Jonas and I examined it quite a long time after Uncle's death. Jonas knew how to open it. I hadn't known until he showed me. There were a few letters in it then, which I turned over to you, Marjorie, together with other material for the biography. None of those letters related to either this man Norris, or the honor fund. Please ring for Jonas, Leslie. He may know of another secret drawer here. I surely do not." Miss Susanna looked nonplussed.

"Who is, or, more likely was, the man Norris to whom he intrusted the matter?" Leslie asked in her keen fashion. "If living, he would be a very old man now."

"I don't know who he is, or was, as the case may he," Miss Hamilton replied, a note of distress in her answer. "According to Uncle Brooke's notes he is, or was, a lawyer. I know of no lawyer, however, by the name of Norris, who was practicing law in the town of Hamilton at that time." She shook a puzzled head.

Jonas just then appearing in the library doorway, Miss Hamilton turned eagerly to him, "Jonas, do you know of another secret drawer here at the Arms besides the one in Uncle Brooke's study desk?"

Jonas came forward without answering the question, his white brows contracted in an evident effort at recollection.

"I don't know *where* there is another secret drawer at the Arms," he said slowly, "but it seems to me I once heard Mr. Brooke speak of one. I can't think now, when, or why, he spoke about it. Maybe it'll come back to me after a while. I only think that he *did* speak of it to me," the old houseman ended with certainty.

"Marjorie found Uncle Brooke's notebook; the one he lost, and worried about losing." Miss Hamilton held up the little black book, relating to Jonas in an excited voice the circumstances of the finding and the important information it contained concerning the "Honor Fund."

Jonas's fine old features registered marked surprise. "*He* talked to me about that honor fund, different times," he said, an excited note in his own voice. "He must have put his idea through, or he wouldn't have written that in the notebook."

"Do you recall a lawyer in Hamilton by the name of Norris, Jonas?" Miss Susanna had fixed hopeful eyes on Jonas.

"No," Jonas answered after due deliberation. "I never heard Mr. Brooke mention any such man, either. He must have lived there, though, or in some near-by town. Mr. Brooke said in the note you just read me that he was going to this man Norris's office the next day to see him."

"Yes," the old lady nodded, "I wish you to go to Hamilton town this afternoon, Jonas, and see John Saxe. He knows everybody in the town and around it. Ask him to look up this man Norris, if he can, as soon as possible. It was his business to write me concerning this trust directly after Uncle Brooke's death. Possibly he thought I knew the situation regarding it. Nevertheless, he should have communicated with me, at any rate. He must have been living then. If he had died before Uncle Brooke died Uncle would have made a new arrangement with another lawyer about the fund."

"Perhaps he may have done so, and any data which might relate to the change of lawyers is in the secret drawer, too," Marjorie suggested.

"And we haven't the remotest idea of where that mysterious secret drawer may be!" Miss Susanna's small hands went up in a despairing gesture.

"Some Chinese puzzle," Leslie commented.

"Maybe the secret drawer is somewhere in the Chinese room," came as a sudden inspiration from Marjorie, prompted by Leslie's mention of the word "Chinese."

"It may be there." Miss Hamilton cast a half startled glance at her companions. "The room has a number of odd Oriental stands and cabinets, any one of them might easily contain a secret drawer. To find it, though!" Up went her hands again. "A needle-in-the-haystack search, I'm afraid. I know less about the Chinese room than any other room in the house. Jonas is far more familiar with it than I. You'll have to be chief hunter, there, Jonas."

"I guess I will." Jonas looked pleased at being thus appointed to the search.

"One thing is certain. The secret drawer *must* be found. It is somewhere in this house which narrows down the area to be searched to the few rooms Uncle Brooke continually used,—his bedroom, his study, the Chinese room and the library. Of the four, I should say the library is the least likely to contain it. The only piece of furniture in here that might contain it is the library table. I doubt the possibility of there being a secret drawer in it."

Miss Susanna rose, went over to the massive, claw-legged mahogany table, and began a slow prowl about it, her sharp eyes taking in its every detail. Jonas had already begun the search, tapping the sides of the table as he peered along the carvings of them for what might prove to be a cunningly concealed spring. He opened the drawers of the table, subjecting the inside of them to the same careful examination.

"There's no secret drawer in this table," was his opinion, spoken at the end of his methodical investigation.

"I'm satisfied, too, there isn't," agreed the mistress of the Arms. "Tomorrow, Jonas, we will tackle the study. There may be another secret drawer in the study desk besides the one of which we know. This afternoon I want you to go to Hamilton and see what you can learn regarding Lawyer Norris. If we should be lucky enough to find the secret drawer within the next few days it won't be necessary to start an investigation, regarding the fifty thousand dollars involved in this affair. The one note plainly states Uncle Brooke's intention of offering a fifty thousand dollar honorarium to Hamilton College under certain conditions, laid down by him. The note of later date states that he completed some sort of arrangement for it with Lawyer Norris. As a trust fund the fifty thousand would have, probably, been deposited in bank at once by Norris. Uncle Brooke used the Hamilton Trust largely, although he was a depositor in several New York City banks. If he gave his check for the honor fund to Norris, together with instructions to him to deposit the check, it may be the Hamilton Bank was used for the transaction. In such case the bank should have the record of the transaction. If so, why was I not notified of it soon after Uncle Brooke's death?" Miss Susanna's question was asked with hurt belligerence.

"An arrangement entire separate from your kinsman's other financial affairs may have been made by him with Norris," Leslie hazarded. "His notes state his confidence in Norris. No doubt then he made the check out to Norris. Of course he might have given him bonds instead."

"He had no bonds at the time he sent for Norris. His large fortune was almost all in cash or in real estate. His father left him a great deal of land, in and about Hamilton, and Hamilton Estates. I'd prefer not to call the Hamilton Trust into the matter, though we may find it necessary in the long run to do so."

"Surely, if the Hamilton Bank had been asked to handle the check you would have heard something about the matter, either directly, or indirectly, during all the years you have lived at the Arms," was Leslie's further opinion.

"I'm inclined to that view of it, too. I doubt if the Hamilton Bank is in any way concerned in this Norris business."

"Why not let my father investigate for you?" proposed Leslie. "He's coming to Hamilton to see me for a day or two, soon after he lands. If, by that time, you haven't found the secret drawer, then please let my father help you in the matter, Miss Susanna," Leslie earnestly petitioned.

"Peter? I never once thought of him!" Miss Susanna exclaimed, brightening visibly. "He's the very man I need to help me. I should be eternally grateful to him, if he would."

"He will," Leslie promised.

"There's more to this than appears on the surface." Miss Hamilton's lips set themselves in severe line. "Granted we find the secret drawer, the finding of the data relating to the honor fund may only serve to prove treachery to his trust on Lawyer Norris's part. As heir to my uncle's fortune and estate, Hamilton Arms, he at least owed it to me to inform me of the trust Uncle Brooke had reposed in him."

"Possibly he was under the impression that you knew of the fifty-thousand dollar fund through your uncle, and had been instructed by Mr. Brooke to assume the responsibility of choosing 'the one' in the event of his death," Marjorie made meditative suggestion. "In such case, he might wait for you to communicate with him regarding it."

"I'll admit such a contingency," the old lady conceded rather reluctantly. "We're all at sea in the matter, it seems. Either Norris, or else the secret drawer, must be found; both preferably."

"This much seems certain, Lawyer Norris was not commissioned by Mr. Brooke to choose 'the one' in the event of Mr. Brooke's decease," Marjorie said.

"I'm not so sure of that." Miss Susanna showed inclination toward distrust of the lawyer. "Uncle Brooke never did things by halves. You must remember, this particular transaction was made less than two years before his death. He was then over eighty years old. He knew his end was near. He had often said as much to me. I believe he would have appointed me to choose 'the one'; not the man Norris. I knew Uncle; his hopes, dreams; ideals, and he knew that I knew them. I can't understand why he did not confide in me at the time he formulated a definite plan." Her voice trembled a trifle on the last words, the manifestation of a hurt spirit.

"I've no doubt but that the lost papers may hold an explanation of that," Marjorie advanced comfortingly, "and they're tucked away somewhere in this very house. Somehow, I have faith in Lawyer Norris. Mr. Brooke would not have chosen him for such an important responsibility if he hadn't been sure of his truth and honor.

"Uncle Brooke's staunchest advocate." Miss Susanna drew Marjorie, standing beside her, into the circle of an arm. "If neither the papers, nor Lawyer Norris should be found, I could still carry out his wish. The important point to be considered, after all, would not be the fifty thousand dollars. The finding of 'the one' would be the real problem, except—" her eyes came to rest with luminous tenderness upon the lovely face bent seriously upon her,—"the one has already been found. I found her for Uncle Brooke, long ago, not far from my gates. She helped a very cranky old lady pick up an overturned basket of plant pots, and showed her how beautiful girlhood might be. Afterward, I came to know her better, not only as a friend, but as an inspiration to Uncle Brooke's college, giving her best to it because of her appreciation of its founder. He chose the motto 'Her ways led upward toward the stars,' as applicable to 'the one.' Without knowing it I chose the same motto as best suited to Marjorie. It is almost as though I had received his direct approval of my choice."

CHAPTER XVI

LESLIE'S QUEER PROBLEM

"And is it yourself, and no other? Is it not time you put in an appearance at the Hall with many apologies for having forgotten us?" Leila Harper ushered Marjorie into her room, her smiling lips in decided apposition to her severe tone.

"It is myself, and, may I ask, who else might it be?" Marjorie retorted as she and Leila enthusiastically wrung hands.

"Ask me nothing. I am that glad to see you, I have no flip answer at my tongue's end. We have all been busy, it would seem. I have been at the Playhouse, with only the typewriter for company, pounding out the parts for my opening play. Midget was invited to become co-editor with Jane Everest on the 'Campus Echo.' Leslie is wrestling with a queer problem of her own. You will hear more about it this evening. And Hamilton Arms has held you a willing captive. We should have come to see you in the evening, except that we have had callers here every night for a week. The Bertramites dinner at Baretti's ended my social rush for a while. I shall begin to lead the life of a hermit for the next three weeks."

"You can't. Miss Susanna had ordered yours and Vera's presence at the Arms at seven o'clock dinner tomorrow night. You are to bring Kathie, Lucy, Lillian and Doris with you. You are to tear them away from any engagements they may have made. Goldendede has something important to tell the Travelers. Robin and Phil are coming, too. I've already 'phoned them."

"Now what has happened?" Leila cocked her head inquisitively to one side. "This much I can guess. Leslie knows all about it. When I asked her for news of the Arms last night, knowing that she had lunched there yesterday, she had little to say except that the library looked fine, and Miss Susanna was well. I saw mystery in the tail of her eye. But I am so polite. I said nothing to her about it." Leila gave Marjorie a drolly hopeful glance.

"I tell you a tiny little bit, Leila Greatheart," Marjorie conceded indulgently. "Something happened yesterday at the Arms that was in the nature of an astonishing surprise. Leslie was there when it happened. Goldendede wishes the girls she has invited to dinner to hear about it. She intends to tell them."

Marjorie felt the color rising in her cheeks. Her own surprise at the finding of Brooke Hamilton's notebook had been secondary to that of Miss Hamilton's avowed choice of "the one." To cover her sudden feeling of confusion she asked hastily, "Where is Vera?"

"Now you are asking me something. Midget is at the freshie frolic. It's tonight, you know, and seems a very clannish affair. There were more than enough sophs to go round. No juniors or seniors were invited this year to help on escort duty. Midget was asked to be one of the three judges of the beauty contest. She, Doris and Calista Wilmot are the fateful trio. The contest was to be held at nine-thirty, so Midget will be here before you go."

"There's a freshie at the dormitory who ought to win it," Marjorie declared with enthusiasm. "I don't know her name, but I do know she is a beauty. I happened to be over at the dorm the day she arrived. She actually took my breath. She has violet blue eyes and curly black auburn hair, and the *sweetest* face, with a skin like a roseleaf."

"I've met her. Her name is Carol Burke. The dorms are hoping she'll win the contest. They say, though, that she will be awfully upset, if she should win it; that she's very shy, and retiring, with but little idea of her own good looks. That is the way you were, Beauty, when I dragged you into the first contest." Leila flashed Marjorie one of her inimitable smiles.

"I remember I felt awfully cross with you because of it," Marjorie reminded. "Now, in my settled old age, I can afford to smile over it."

"But if you were to walk into the gym tonight in your violet dress you would win it again," Leila predicted.

"My violet dress!" Marjorie hurried away from the subject of the contest. "It seems strange, Leila, but it looks as lovely as ever; not a bit old style. Captain shortened it and took out the sleeves, and now it's a dream. How are the Bertramites? I must have them over at the Rest soon to dinner."

"They are—" Two deliberate, successive knocks on the door sent Leila scurrying to open it for Leslie, who had dropped Marjorie at the Hall and had then gone on to the garage with her roadster.

"Come on into my room for a while," Leslie invited. "Marjorie hasn't seen Fifteen since it was done over. Jewel Marie is gaily fox-trotting at the frolic, thank goodness, and we can discuss the affairs of the universe in peace. Leave a scrawl on the table for Vera when she comes in, Leila. Have you seen Miss Remson yet?" she turned to Marjorie.

"Yes; only for a moment. She had to go to town on unexpected business. I'll run over tomorrow to see her. Goldendede wants her to be at the dinner tomorrow night."

"'Tis done. '*Midget, Attention!* Come to Fifteen. No knocking necessary,'" Leila read out, then gave the penned message a vigorous drying fluttering before running it through with a long, black-headed pin, and sticking the pin into the middle of the study table.

Leslie closed the door of Fifteen behind her comrades to the tune of admiring exclamation from Marjorie.

"Can this celostrous cozy corner be old Fifteen?" Marjorie's face glowed appreciation of Leslie's artistry.

"It can be. It is." Leslie showed her pleasure of Marjorie's lively approval of her color scheme and arrangement. "I liked it a little better before I changed things around in order to make room for Miss Ogden," she said.

"I am still wondering at your cleverness, and also at how it came about that you gathered in the homeless Miss Ogden," Leila said a trifle inquisitively. "Now tell me nothing." She put up her hand, laughing as though to ward off an unsolicited confidence. "I am not as inquisitive as I seem."

"I'm still wondering myself how I happened to drag in that kid," Leslie confessed, smiling. "She was no end disappointed because she couldn't find a campus room. I'm only going to be here till Christmas. It seemed so selfish in me to bar the midget out. I've a sort of plan going in my head about Fifteen—something I'd like to do with it when I leave here to go to a real home."

"What, Leslie?" Marjorie was all interest.

"I'm going to will my half of Fifteen to the first girl on the dormitory waiting list. If she doesn't want it, then the next on the list will do. It will be a free proposition, same as the dormitory, but with all the comfy advantages that being on the campus means."

"Your plan is just like you, Leslie. It's lovely," Marjorie accorded with quiet sincerity.

"You are a noble Cairns, and I think well of you," Leila spoke lightly, but Leslie understood the undercurrent of earnestness in the speech. The Irish girl was wondering, however, what the effect of the carrying out of Leslie's plan would be upon Miss Ogden. She suspected her of being a social climber which would not accord at all with Leslie's scheme of things.

As though reading her mind, Leslie remarked speculatively, "I am going to talk to Miss Ogden about Fifteen. I haven't yet explained it to her. I hardly believe she will make any objection to it when I finally tell her. That will be shortly before I leave here for Carden Hedge."

Watching Leslie's face Marjorie glimpsed the shadow of the old dominating leader who had ruled the frivolous San Soucians by sheer determined will.

"Do you like Miss Ogden, Leslie?" sprang impulsively from her lips. Immediately she became vexed with herself for having unthinkingly asked so personal a question. "I shouldn't have asked you that," she apologized quickly.

"Glad you did. It's given me an opening to speak my mind to you and Leila about her, and also this crowd of freshies from New York who are at the Hall. You ask me if I like Miss Ogden. Yes, and no. At heart she's a democrat. Outwardly, she's a goose, with snobbish aspirations. She'll need more than one jolt to wake her up to herself, and she's in a fair way soon to gather in the first one. The New York freshies are snobs, Marjorie; same type as the Sans. Leila, Vera and I discovered as much the day we first met them. The Ogden kid is wild about them; has a crush on Miss Norris, the banner snob of the gang. Experience is a great teacher! I understand this bunch of high hats. She doesn't. I can't very well warn her against them. They're her classmates. She would probably resent such a warning, as a meddlesome interference on my part. Still, I hate to see her hurt without having first done what I can to prevent calamity. Leila, Vera and I have been keeping a starboard eye upon her, trying diplomatically to steer her clear of snags. We decided we'd best consult you about her, Marvelous Manager." Leslie's eyes rested expectantly upon Marjorie.

"Why underrate your own superior capabilities?" Marjorie glanced from Leila to Leslie with twinkling eyes.

"We are but poor playhouse managers, and, at that, far from marvelous. It is one thing to manage mummers, in a make-believe drama. They are pleased to be managed. But to attempt to manage freshies, in a real drama, who have no taste for being managed, is quite another." Leslie made a deprecatory gesture. "These New York freshies, Beauty, are an innovation at Hamilton. They are a gay, noisy set in their rooms, going back and forth to them through their end of the hall with plenty of laughter and commotion. To the other students at the Hall they show small friendliness. Miss Ogden loses no opportunity to court favor with them. We know they make sport of her behind her back, for we have heard them sneer about her. They patronize her to her face. Why they do not snub her outright, as they have two or three of the sophs at the Hall, we wondered, until yesterday. Then we heard that at the freshie class meeting she nominated Miss Norris, their leader, for president. Now we shall see what we shall see," Leila said significantly.

"Was Miss Norris elected president?" Marjorie inquired interestedly.

"Yes; her crowd had been busily electioneering for her. She won over Miss Foster of Acasia House by only two votes. Her roommate, Miss Taylor, gave a dinner for her last night at Baretti's."

"Was Miss Ogden invited?" Marjorie's interest had deepened.

"Yes! I was glad to hear from Leslie that she was."

"She had Miss Taylor to thank for it," Leslie interposed. "If any other girl in that crowd had given it, I'll say Jewel Marie wouldn't have had a look in. This Miss Taylor is rather different from the others. She's stout and sleepy-looking. She appears stodgy until one happens to see her laugh. When she laughs, and that's not often, her whole face changes. One sees humor written on every feature. She'd make a wonderful Touchstone in 'As You Like It.'"

"Yes, and Miss Norris would make a fine Henry the Fifth. I'm thinking of putting it on at the Playhouse this winter. Still, she is one I am not anxious to manage. I am not fond of wrangling," Leila made a wry face, "and I have heard her differ, far from politely, with the girls of her own set."

"It's this way, Marjorie," Leslie broke in seriously, "Miss Norris at first almost ignored Miss Ogden. All of a sudden, she became quite gracious to her; she lunched Miss Ogden at the Colonial and invited her into the sacred precincts of her room a couple of times. Jewel Marie nearly expired with joy. She would have followed her crush about like a faithful terrier, if I hadn't kept her busy trotting around with me. Leila and I both predicted that the bubble would burst soon after election. Since then Miss Ogden has twice invited Miss Norris to dinner at Baretti's. On both occasions she has disappointed the kid at the last minute with flimsy excuses. She's still fatuously blind, and the eye-opening process is going to be some shock to her. I'm tempted to let her hear me out, straight from the shoulder, then let her rave. By the time she finds herself dropped by her crush she'll be able to meet the terrible blow without making herself ridiculous." There was a suspicion of good-humored scorn in Leslie's voice. "She isn't remarkably tactful. She's more likely to go up in the air over the snub, just because of her hurt feelings."

"I believe I'd try the straight-from-the-shoulder tactics, Leslie," was Marjorie's thoughtful advice. "Miss Ogden may be angry with you, at first, but she will understand afterward that you were trying to help her. It will prepare her in a measure for what you believe is going to happen, even though she should resent your warning at the time it is given."

"I'll have a talk with her in the morning," Leslie nodded with decision. "She was planning on having a good time tonight. I'm not going to spoil pleasant memories of it by croaking. Miss Felton took her to the frolic."

"Oh, I remember *her*. She is the pretty, brown-haired girl who was the first to protest against the petition Miss Ferguson started on that memorable night last spring here at the Hall," Marjorie said with a reminiscent smile.

"She's a mighty nice girl," Leslie returned, "and I wish, for her own sake, that this misguided roommate of mine had a crush on Miss Felton. Muriel's show was a greater success than she thought it might be. The sophs at the Hall, who joined the Lotus Club as freshies, are a congenial crowd this year, with the exception of Miss Ferguson. She has attached herself to the New York crowd, and is very pally with Miss Norris. I daresay the N. Y.'s know my past campus history better than I do," Leslie declared with grim satire. "They try to ignore my existence whenever they can, for which I thank them."

"Wait until my theatre article appears next week in the 'Echo.' Then you will suddenly see a great change among them. What girl does not love the idea of acting? Leila and I will then be ranked as desirable acquaintances rather than antiquated P. G.'s," Leslie humorously prophesied.

Mention of the Playhouse turned the conversation from Leslie's "misguided" roommate into a more pleasing channel. Leila had decided to open the theatre with an elaborate performance of "The Merchant of Venice." She proposed next to follow the Shakespearean drama with a revue, then, later, to present her new Irish play, "The Leprachaun." After the holidays she hoped to put on "Henry the Fifth," provided she could secure a cast to suit her critical fancy.

"It will be no trick to find a cast for the Merchant of Venice," she told her interested companions. "Doris will add to her campus fame as Portia, Gussie will make an ideal Antonio, and Miss Duncan will cover herself with glory in playing Shylock. On Bassonio, I have not yet decided. I may ask Miss Taylor, the stout freshman, to play the part. She is tall enough, and broad enough of shoulder, to play a man's part well." Leila glanced questioningly from one to the other of her chums. "She interests me, and, incidentally, it may lead to a better state of affairs here at the Hall. I suspect her of having some influence upon her crowd. They babble like brooks when together, but she, I have noticed, says little, though her oddly pale blue eyes miss nothing."

"Don't ever talk to me again about marvelous managing," Marjorie exclaimed. "*You* are the real Marvelous Manager. You've picked up a trail to a better state of affairs here, already. Go ahead; ask Miss Taylor to—"

The unexpected violent opening of the door cut off Marjorie's unfinished sentence. Three pairs of eyes suddenly directed themselves at the tempestuous entrant. A very small girl in a peachblow-hued evening frock had fairly bounced into the room, banging the door behind her.

CHAPTER XVII

WHAT HAPPENED AT THE FROLIC

"Hello, Jewel," Leslie calmly greeted after a quick glance at the freshman's anger-dark features.

Without answering the angry girl dashed across the room to her couch bed, flinging herself upon it. Her doubled fists began beating an enraged tattoo upon the pillows, to which her slippered feet kicked themselves in time upon the couch cover. "Oh, oh, oh!" she repeatedly ejaculated in rage-thickened tones. "I'll never forgive her! Oh, oh, oh!"

The trio of silent spectators to the freshman's gust of anger could not but exchange significant glances. Into the mind of each had sprung the question: "Had the blow, which Leslie had anticipated, fallen already?"

"Let us go into my room," Leila proposed tactfully, rising from her chair as she spoke.

"We'll wait for you there, Leslie." Marjorie was already following Leila to the door.

"Go ahead." Leslie's dark brows raised themselves in indicative despair. "I'll join you presently."

"I'm wondering if the prophecy has come true so soon," were Leila's first words as they shut themselves into her room. "Sit down, Beauty, and be at home." Abruptly she dropped into a chair and burst into laughter.

"Never think that I am making a mock of misfortune," she said presently, a mirthful quiver in her tones. "I'm still thinking of the amazing bounce that midget made into the room. It might well have been that of a circus performer. She little knows the honor in store for her. It seems I have found a star for my play 'The Leprechaun' and that without the trouble of seeking."

"You are a funny old dear, Leila Harper," Marjorie, girl-like, could not do other than laugh with Leila. "Something harrowing must have happened to Miss Ogden at the frolic to send her away from it in such a tempest. It's early yet." Her eyes sought the clock on Leila's dressing-table. "Only twenty-five minutes to ten. The beauty contest must just have begun. She's awfully tiny, isn't she?" she again reverted to the subject of Miss Ogden, "at least two inches shorter than Vera. She's pretty, I think."

"She has the prettiness of a child when she is good-natured," Leila said, "but, oh, my stars, what a temper! Until tonight she has shown nothing of it to Leslie, Vera and me. Vera will not be long in coming now. She promised to slip away from the gym as soon as the contest was over. Grant that before then Leslie will have calmed the storm and reduced the whirlwind to order," she finished with dry humor.

It was Vera, however, who appeared in the room ahead of Leslie. She dropped into a chair with exaggerated weariness and a long, sighing: "*Such* a time as there has been tonight, over at the gym. Truly, girls, it was dreadful! Where's Leslie?" Vera's quick glance in the direction of Leslie's room conveyed an inkling of the reason of Leslie's absence.

"Yes; she is in Fifteen with Miss Ogden," Leila interpreted the glance, and answered. "Now, for goodness' sake, Midget, are we to know what it is all about?"

"You are; and this is the tale. There was a *positive tongue* battle in the gym tonight, just before the beginning of the beauty contest. It looked for a minute as though there might be some actual hand-to-hand fighting done." Vera gave a faint little chuckle. "The trouble started as the result of an accident to Miss Norris's gown. During the last fox-trot before the beginning of the beauty walk, Miss Norris was standing near the punch bowl corner, drinking lemonade. The floor of the gym was as slippery as glass. The sophs had put too much wax on it, and there'd been a lot of slipping and sliding done. The girls were having a lot of fun because of it. Miss Ogden and a tall soph, whose name I don't know yet, were doing a very frisky variation of the trot. The punch bowl was one of those thin lovely tinted glass affairs and stood on a stand the sophs had fixed up and draped with the class colors. Miss Ogden and the soph were going it full speed. In the first place, the stand had been set too far from the wall. Just as the two girls came close to it, Miss Ogden's feet slipped and the pair crashed into the stand. Over went stand and punch bowl, *simply deluging* Miss Norris with lemonade." Vera's hands went up in horrified recollection of the scene.

"Was ever anything more unfortunate?" Leila turned to Marjorie.

"*Dreadfully*," Marjorie agreed. She found herself suddenly sympathizing with the small, rage-swept figure she had seen for a moment in Leslie's room.

"It was an accident. The majority of the girls at the frolic would have accepted it as such, without being peeved, if it had happened to any one of them. Miss Norris was furious over it. It was too bad, of course. She had on a perfectly ducky white satin frock. She really looked beautiful in it, though I think her beauty is of a cold, arrogant type. She is evidently high-tempered, and she lost control of her temper. She fairly screamed out at Miss Ogden: '*You've ruined my dress, you rough, ill-bred little bounder.*' This, while Miss Ogden was apologizing to her for the accident, and half crying. The beauty line had just begun to form. A good many of the girls fell out of line, mostly the freshies, and hurried over to the wreck. The punch bowl was smashed to smithereens and the stand lay in a big puddle of lemonade. The silk draping was soaked with it. The judges' platform wasn't more than a dozen feet away from the smash so we could hear a part of what was being said by the two girls.

"I felt sorry for Miss Ogden. She tried to keep her temper, even after Miss Norris had spoken so insultingly to her. She merely clenched her hands and repeated: 'I'm more sorry than I can say, Miss Norris; I'm more than ready to pay for your damaged gown. I know it's imported, but I'll be glad to—' Miss Norris answered in the most hateful way, '*You*—You show your ill-breeding in suggesting such a thing. You are simply impossible.'

"Miss Ogden couldn't stand that so she blazed out: '*You* didn't seem to regard me as impossible when you asked me to electioneer for you. *You*, not *I*, are ill-bred!' Miss Norris positively shrieked, '*How dare you insult me*? You know you haven't spoken truthfully.' Six or seven of Miss Norris's crowd joined in then, and they all turned upon Miss Ogden. Then there began such a chorus of gabbling, I couldn't distinguish much that was being said. Some of Miss Ogden's friends joined the fuss and began to defend *her*. She was in the middle of the crowd, wild with rage, telling them all what she thought of them. The whole fuss hardly occupied more than five minutes' time. Miss Elgin, the soph president, hurried over to me and said: 'Come and help me stop this fuss, *please*, Miss Mason. It's disgraceful!' I told her to come up on the platform and order the beauty line to reform instantly, saying that, otherwise, the contest would be declared off."

Vera laughed softly. "You should have seen the mob break up. Five minutes later the line was strolling around the gym, as decorously as could be. I don't know what became of either Miss Norris, or Miss Ogden. Neither was in the beauty line, naturally. Most of Miss Norris's crowd were. It sounds uncharitable, but I'm convinced that Miss Norris hoped to win in the contest. She wouldn't have, though, even if her gown hadn't been damaged. Miss Burke, a dormitory freshie, won it. She was the most beautiful girl in the line. The dorms gave her a great send-off. I beat it for the Hall the moment after Doris delivered the adjuration to Beauty, but I could still hear the girls cheering until I was half way across the campus."

"Miss Ogden is in her room. Leslie is with her," Leila informed Vera. "She came in in a fine flurry. We fled, knowing we had best leave her to Leslie."

"She has my sympathy. It was not only ill-bred, but also unkind in Miss Norris to make such a scene because of an accident," was Vera's slightly contemptuous opinion. "If this fuss had occurred before the class election she would never have won the presidential vote."

"She's made a bad start at Hamilton," Marjorie said soberly. "She's taken the wrong road, and no one but herself can put her on the right one again. If only she could be made to see it."

"It is like you, Beauty, to mourn over the ill-doer, and for that we have loved you. Leslie is what she is today because you believed she had a better self. It is yet too young in the college year to say what beneficial changes may come, if any, to Miss Norris. If she has a better self," Leila's tone had become sceptical, "I am afraid she will be put to considerable trouble to find it. I know I shall take no pains to point it out to her."

"Shall you ask her to be in Henry the Fifth after what happened tonight?" Marjorie inquired half mischievously.

"*Now* you *are* asking me something." Leila's wide smile broke out. "I might be doing better were I to ask her to play 'Kate' in 'The Taming of the Shrew.'"

The entrance of Leslie into the room turned the attention of the three girls in her direction.

"What happened at the gym, Vera?" she asked as she drew a chair forward and joined the group.

"Then she hasn't yet come out of it?" Vera opened questioning blue eyes.

"Oh, she has, to the extent of saying there was a scrap at the gym, and that she hates Miss Norris. That's the part she keeps on emphasizing to me. She's so sore over whatever happened tonight at the gym that she can't see straight. She promised to spill the news to me tomorrow. I didn't stop to quiz her about it. I thought you'd know, perhaps."

Vera recounted briefly what she had already told Leila and Marjorie.

"*Good night,*" was Leslie's slangily forceful reception of Vera's account of the evening's accident. "No wonder the kid is sore. Some one ought to send Miss Norris a book of etiquette for social occasions with a few choice paragraphs underlined. Leave it to Muriel to do it, if she were here. I wonder if Miss Norris is worse than I used to be?" she pondered aloud. "I believe she *is*. I doubt if, in the same circumstances, I'd have raised a commotion in public about getting a lemonade shower-bath. Of course, it was the beauty contest that started her going. She'll never forgive Jewel Marie for being the means of snapping her out of it. The kid says she hates Miss Norris. It looks as though internal war might ramp and rage at Wayland Hall, unless someone with scads of nerve should rise in her might, and put the kibosh on it."

"You've always said *you* had more nerve than anybody else, Leslie," Marjorie laughed, yet there was a gleam of earnestness in her brown eyes.

"Yep; I know it. I was just thinking about that myself." Leslie's eyes met Marjorie's in a glance of slow significance.

"While you and Beauty find a plan to make the Hall a safe place for two timid old ladies like Midget and me to live in, I shall brew you a cup of tea, and Midget must lay the plates and bring out the cakes."

Leila and Vera immediately began to busy themselves with the preparation of a spread, leaving Marjorie and Leslie to the discussion which had seemingly narrowed down to they two.

"This crowd of Miss Norris's are doing their level best to upset the democratic peace of Wayland Hall," Leslie said emphatically. "They can't possibly win in the long run, but they can keep things here disagreeably stirred up, perhaps all year, unless their activities are nipped in the bud. Last year Muriel's show turned the tide in my favor when Miss Ferguson and Dulcie Vale tried to down me. There was a greater number of girls in the Orchid Club, too. There are twelve of these freshies. One may safely count Mildred Ferguson in with them. Thirteen disturbers to vanquish. Go to it Cairns II. That's how I feel about it. That's what Peter the Great would say, if I told *him* my troubles."

"You have the same determined spirit I can imagine Brooke Hamilton as having had," Marjorie reached out, laying a warmly sympathetic hand upon one of Leslie's. "If I were still living at the Hall as a P. G., you know I would fight shoulder to shoulder with you. But I'm not far away from you. Remember, if you need my help in any way, it shall be yours."

"You certainly have some imagination." Leslie indulged in one of her oddly silent laughs. "Thank you for the Brooke Hamilton bouquet, and I'll know where to come running, if things begin to speed up too much for me."

"Do you believe these freshies are interested in Hamilton as their Alma Mater?" Marjorie put the question after a meditative silence.

"No; not even a little bit. They're of the present-moment flapper type, indifferent to everything but their own pleasure. They spend their recreation hours mostly in their cars. They're not the sort to respond to friendly advances. They've been fairly pleasant with the other freshies here. Now that freshie class election is over—" Leslie's shrug was indicative of her meaning.

"You and Leila are both so clever, Leslie, and you two practically control campus dramatics. If only you could win these girls over by offering them parts in the plays to be given at the Playhouse this winter. It might make them feel more in touch with Hamilton, and awaken in them a new spirit of college interest." Marjorie's suggestion rang with her own boundless enthusiasm toward Hamilton.

"Something like that," Leslie nodded. "Frankly, Marjorie, that New York freshie crowd bores me silly. So does Jewel Marie, at times. But she's of the people, all democrat underneath her ridiculous idea of caste. I can see where I'm going to run into trouble if I don't watch my step while trying to win over a bunch of girls that she's down on. Just the same, Mrs. Macy," Leslie purposely took on Jerry's matter-of-fact tone, "*it will have to be done. Yes siree; it will have to be done,* and it's up to Cairns II to tackle it, *and get away with it.*"

CHAPTER XVIII

A SENTIMENTAL INTEREST

"And you say John Saxe doesn't know who owns those Kenton Street properties. That's strange." Peter Cairns' alert dark features registered a mixture of surprise and doubt. "He should know."

"I'm convinced that he doesn't," Hal Macy returned. "He told me the owner of them transacted all business pertaining to them through an agent, who refused to tell him the owner's name. The agent told Mr. Saxe that the owner was not keen about selling them, but might consider one hundred, fifty thousand for them."

"Ridiculous. I wouldn't give a penny over forty thousand for them, and that's a very fair figure," the financier declared with slightly contemptuous finality.

"I offered fifty thousand for them, through Saxe. I hardly thought them worth more than that. The site is worth far more than are the houses. They are ramshackle, with practically no modern conveniences. It has been my idea to buy them, have the houses torn down, and, in their stead, erect modern two-story dwellings with all modern conveniences. These properties extend along the south side of the street for almost two blocks. The families who live in the rickety houses have been there for years, and are among the really deserving poor of Hamilton. As a staid, conservative college town Hamilton has little commercial or industrial interest. There is little work for the laboring man in and about the town at present. The shutting down of two or three of the few manufactories in Hamilton has made wage-earning a problem. I have talked with some of these poor fellows and have found their conditions deplorable. With no steady work, and a high rental to pay, to say nothing of the present high cost of living, the majority of them are hard pressed. I should like, at least, to see them in comfortable houses, at a more moderate rental than they are now obliged to pay."

Hal's eyes had strayed from Peter Cairns' strong face to that of his Violet girl, confident of her sympathetic approval. They two, Leila and Vera, Leslie and her father had dined that evening at the Arms with Miss Susanna and were now gathered in the library for a confidential session.

Peter Cairns had arrived in Hamilton on the day before and was Miss Susanna's guest. He had come in prompt response to her letter containing the affectionate mandate, "Peter, I want you to drop everything else and come to the Arms. I must see you." Hal, still hugging his mysterious secret to his heart, had been equally anxious to see the financier. He had also pinned his faith upon Peter Cairns to ascertain for him the identity of the owner of the properties.

Listening to the discussion between Miss Susanna and the financier regarding the possibilities of locating Lawyer Norris, if living, or of obtaining the much desired information regarding the fifty-thousand-dollar Honor Fund should the attorney be deceased, Hal was more than ever convinced of Peter Cairns' brilliant capabilities. His terse assurance: "I'll attend to it for you, Miss Susanna, though it may take a little time to trace Norris," had served to strengthen Hal's belief in him.

"And *that* is the surprise you've been hiding from me," Marjorie's face was radiant. "I love it, and you, too, bushels and bushels," she finished childishly.

"I knew you would." Hal's answering smile was like a caress. He tore his eyes reluctantly from his wife's lovely face to explain boyishly to the others, "I'm a man without a job, you know, and it worries me, as much, maybe, as being out of work worries those poor fellows on Kenton Street. The only difference between us is that of money. They haven't enough. I have too much. My grandfather left me a whole lot of money. A great uncle of mine left me a lot more. I'd like to use some of it to help the other fellow. Marjorie and I are so happy, I'd like to see others happy, too, because of it. I can't see being a country gentleman with a stable full of fine horses, hunting dogs, and all that sort of thing. I want to keep going, in a way that will benefit others. Marjorie taught me the glory of work. Now I'd like best of all to show her how well I've learned my lesson."

"Hal!" Came a flash of white, and Marjorie had perched herself upon the arm of Hal's chair, her soft lips pressed against his cheek, a bare, clinging arm about his neck.

"You have your reward," Peter Cairns said gallantly. Unconsciously his eyes strayed past the married lovers to Leila. Happening to meet the financier's glance, Leila felt the color rise in her cheeks. She instantly looked away, self-vexed. Their glances had merely chanced to meet, was her annoyed thought. Deep in her heart, however, she was conscious of a growing admiration for the clean-cut, keen-eyed finance king.

Leslie, always a close observer, had missed neither the exchange of glances nor the quick-leaping color to Leila's cheeks. She smiled to herself, as though vastly amused by some sudden amusing thought of her own.

"It is the one reward worth gaining." Hal's right arm had wrapped itself about Marjorie's waist.

"You two children have the best," Miss Susanna's brisk intonation had softened to gentleness. "You can well afford to be money-generous. So can

I, for that matter. I'm rich in devoted friends, too. I'd like to join in this welfare enterprise of yours, Hal, if you'll permit me."

"This is the best news I've heard since Marjorie told me that she loved me bushels and bushels." Hal's handsome features were smiling anew.

"Why not let Leslie and me into it, too?" Peter Cairns demanded.

"The Marjorie Dean Macy Welfare Colony," suggested Leslie. "How's that for a name?"

"*No, indeed,*" Marjorie made lively objection. "Either the Susanna Hamilton, or the Peter Cairns Welfare Colony would sound much better."

"Not a bit of it," sturdily objected Miss Susanna. "Leslie has the right idea. We are all here together tonight, the best of friends, because of Marjorie's interest, direct or indirect, in us when we were practically strangers to one another."

"*Ain't it the truth?*" Leslie agreed in a tone of awed wonder that set them all laughing.

"We are really Marjorie's own colony. Don't attempt to deny it, young lady," Miss Hamilton shook a playfully reproving finger at Marjorie, "nor try to disown us."

"As though I could." Marjorie slipped from the arm of Hal's chair and went over to sit on that of Miss Susanna.

"I'll try again," Leslie said humorously. "Since Marjorie and Miss Susanna both object to having our new colony named for them, and I know Peter the Great will object to the honor, the minute he can get a word in, why not call it the Hamilton Colony?"

"Yes; of course, that is so much better," Marjorie laughingly seconded.

"I didn't think you'd go back on me, Leslie." This time Miss Susanna's finger shook itself at Leslie.

"I haven't. I'm only trying to please everybody here, and not getting away with it," Leslie assured with an enjoying grin.

"It all goes back to Mr. Brooke, Goldendede. Hamilton was his native town. If such a condition as Hal has just described to us had existed in Hamilton in his day, he would have tried to remedy it, as we hope to do," Marjorie made soulful argument. "I'd like to think of it as his colony, all of us working together under the inspiring name of Hamilton."

"I'm not proof against such an argument. You know my weak spot, and have taken advantage of it, bad child." Miss Susanna drew Marjorie into the curve of her arm. "Well, we'll see about it. Now let us leave the naming of our colony until later. While Peter goes on the trail of information, Hal shall take us down to Kenton Street for a look at the properties. If only we could find that aggravating secret drawer we could straighten this Honor Fund matter out like magic." She heaved an impatient sigh.

"You will one day find it in the last place you might expect it to be, and that is but poor consolation," Leila prognosticated.

"What I should call encouragement from a purely Celtic standpoint," Vera said teasingly.

"Just like that," Leslie joined Vera in teasing Leila.

"But for these two, I could lead a peaceful life," Leila complained resignedly.

"The three of you had better come over to the Arms on Saturday for the week-end. I'll set you to hunting the secret drawer in separate rooms. Then you won't be disturbed, Leila." Miss Susanna surveyed the trio with twinkling eyes. "I daresay, however, that I'll find the three of you all hob-nobbing cheerfully together in one room before the day is over," she mischievously predicted.

"Something like that *might* happen," Leila conceded with her widest smile, "I am so kind-hearted."

Peter Cairns and Miss Susanna exchanged sympathetically droll glances as they listened to the lively repartee that went on for a little among the three chums.

"The best is ours, Peter," the old lady said softly to him with a quick sidelong nod toward Leslie.

"I know it," was his fervent response as he looked with fond pride at his daughter's laughter-bright face. Again his eyes strayed to Leila who was indulging in what she characterized as "a fit of Irish glee." She and Leslie were evidently the best of friends. He wondered, if, in the dim future, there might come a time when he—. He had been interested in Leila almost since first meeting. He had sternly dismissed the sentimental thought that invariably sprang into his brain each time he saw the clever Irish girl.

"Peter," Miss Susanna's voice broke in upon his nearly sentimental meditation, "I wish you'd come and take a look about the Chinese room. You've traveled in the Orient and know a good deal about the secret ways of the Orientals. Your knowledge of Chinese things may steer you straight to the secret drawer."

"Are we invited to go along?" Marjorie inquired plaintively.

"Of course, goose, we'll all go, and do a little hunting. I believe in making my guests useful," laughed the old lady.

The searchers trooped merrily into the Chinese room, volubly voicing their hope that the financier might hit upon the hiding-place of the secret drawer. For an hour they busied themselves diligently, running their hands over the various pieces of teakwood furniture, and pressing upon spots of it that suggested even remotely the presence of a secret mechanism.

At the end of an hour, however, they had come no nearer to finding the too-well-concealed drawer than when they had begun the search. Even the financier admitted himself as baffled on first hunt.

"I'm coming up to the Hedge before Thanksgiving to get it ready for occupancy. If you haven't found the drawer by that time, I'll have another go at it. Meantime, while I'm hunting Norris, let the girls help you keep up the search here. I have a lively hunch that we shall find Norris, or possibly his heirs, and the drawer, too, *and*," his dark features set themselves with stubborn determination, "I propose to leave nothing undone toward making that hunch come true."

CHAPTER XIX

AN UNSCRUPULOUS PLOTTER

As a result of the agreement Leila, Leslie, Marjorie and Vera had made among themselves on the night of the freshman frolic toward winning over Stephanie Norris and her chums, Leila had decided to open the season at the Playhouse with "Henry the Fifth," rather than "The Merchant of Venice."

It was with no particular pleasure, however, that, on an evening not long after the frolic she knocked upon Miss Norris's door for a polite interview with the difficult freshman, concerning the honor she proposed to extend to her. "And if I should suddenly come flying back here, as though blown down the hall by a strong gale, feel no surprise!" she confided to Vera. "I am not counting upon a cordial reception."

To her surprise, she found the arrogant freshman inclined to be gracious. Stephanie had come into a realization of several pertinent truths since the night of the freshman frolic. One of them was a nettled realization that she had behaved unwisely in flying into a fit of temper with Miss Ogden. Her own particular coterie of chums had sympathized with her, with the exception of Laura Taylor, her roommate. Mildred Ferguson was also on her side. She was not so sure of Mildred's roommate, Miss Watson, who had escorted Laura to the frolic. Laura had voiced frank disapproval of Stephanie's rude outburst when they had reached the privacy of their room after the frolic was over. They had in consequence quarreled hotly and had since been barely upon speaking terms.

The article which had appeared in "The Campus Echo," three days after the frolic, relative to the "Playhouse," had not added to Stephanie's peace of mind. She had not supposed "that horrid Miss Cairns" to be of so much importance on the campus. According to Mildred Ferguson, Miss Cairns had no right, whatever, to be on the campus. Her father's money alone had influenced President Matthews to overlook her many misdemeanors. She had actually been expelled from college, then later had been permitted to return to Hamilton as a matter of favoritism. As Miss Ogden's roommate, she might be expected to sympathize with "the tiresome little creature."

Stephanie was still brimming with rancor against the offending freshman. Thanks to Miss Ogden's stupid clumsiness not only her lovely important gown, but also her high hope of winning the beauty contest had been ruined. She had vengefully determined "to get even" with the diminutive freshman to the point of having already considered various spiteful schemes for humiliating the object of her spite. What she purposed to do, when she had finally hit upon a telling plan of revenge, was to carry it out with a secrecy that should permit of no discovery.

Leila's unexpected call, together with the flattering import of her errand, filled Stephanie with a sense of gratified triumph. She took good care to hide it under a forced pretense of graciousness, however. Her unreasoning dislike for the clever manager of the Playhouse must not be permitted to stand in the way of her own popularity. She had "lost out" wretchedly in the beauty contest. She could not afford any further "flivvers." Nevertheless, she chose to demur over the stellar role which Leila now offered her on the plea that she would like to "think the matter over" before coming to a decision.

Leila presently returned to her own room, not in the least deceived by the scheming freshman, but half sorry she had asked her to take part in the coming Shakespearean play. "The deed is done," she dryly informed Vera as she entered their room. "Let us hope it has not been ill done. I am less than ever taken with Miss Norris. She has little more college spirit than a basket of potatoes."

"How very uncharitable you are," Vera giggled at Leila's disgusted comparison.

"Am I not?" The Irish girl's half-frowning features brightened into a faint grin. She thereupon gave Vera a brief account of her interview with Stephanie, ending with: "I am the willing slave of democracy, but it is a hard master."

With Leila's exit from Stephanie's room, her roommate, Laura Taylor, who had been present during Leila's call, broke the constraint which had hung heavily upon the two since the night of the frolic.

"You are in luck, Steve," she observed with quiet significance. "You can afford to forget about the beauty contest flivver. Something much better has come your way. Go to it. You can act. You ought to make a wonderful King Hal."

"Yes; I *can* act." Stephanie walked over to her mirror, chin raised to a complacent angle. "I hope the costumes for the part are good. If I don't like them, I shall send to a New York costumer's for others that may suit me better."

"Yes?" Behind Stephanie's back Laura's plump shoulders shrugged bored disapproval.

"It's exactly as I told you it would be." Stephanie suddenly swung around from the mirror, speaking with triumphant energy. "Those snippy P. G.'s, Miss Harper and Miss Cairns, simply *had* to recognize my worth. It looks to me as though Miss Harper might be on my side, and not on Miss Ogden's.

Perhaps Miss Cairns has had enough of her, too. Both have no doubt heard about our fuss at the beauty contest."

"Listen to me, Steve," Laura burst forth impatiently, "for goodness' sake stop kidding yourself along. You happen to be the type Miss Harper happened to need for King Henry. *That's* the reason, *and the only reason* why she has offered you the part."

"It is *not*," Stephanie flared back hotly. "You are—"

"Kindly permit me to finish." Laura spoke in a tone which Stephanie recognized and dreaded. It meant that the wall of silence was likely to loom again between them, to remain raised indefinitely.

"*Oh, pardon me*," she apologized with covert sarcasm.

"Neither Miss Harper nor Miss Cairns are the sort to 'take sides' in the way you seem to believe they might. If they were, they would certainly not be on yours. You were far more to blame the other night at the frolic than was Miss Ogden. If you had spoken to me, as you spoke to her, I should have been tempted to make more trouble for you than she made."

"I was *not* to blame. She ruined my gown, then flew at me like a—a tiger," stormed Stephanie.

"But not until you had called her a clumsy idiot, a bounder and various other uncomplimentary names," Laura stolidly reminded. "You owe that girl an apology."

"*I*," Stephanie indicated herself with an outraged fore finger, "*apologize to that miserable little upstart?* I'll never forgive her for having put me in such a humiliating position. I'll find a way to get back at her for it, too. Remember what I say."

"Oh, drop it," Laura commented wearily. "The sooner you live down your part of that fuss, the better off you'll be. And don't come to me with any of your ridiculous revenge schemes. Nothing doing."

"You talk like a prig—like one of those silly dormitory students," Stephanie threw back with supreme contempt. "What has come over you, Laura Taylor? You act entirely different from the good pal you used to be to me." Stephanie cunningly appealed to Laura from a standpoint of loyalty. Laura hated disloyalty.

"I've been loyal to you, if that's what you mean." Laura turned a coolly level gaze upon her friend's petulant features. "Everything at Hamilton is so different from the way things were at prep school—more inspiring, and—" Laura paused, then added reflectively, "worth while."

"Horrors! I hope you haven't enlisted under the reform banner," Stephanie sneered. "It looks fatally like it."

"Don't let it worry you." A quick flush rose to the stout girl's plump cheeks. "Watch your own step. I mean that in good part, Steve."

"*Thank you*," came the disdainful retort. "I *hope* I am capable of managing my own affairs."

"I hope so, too," Laura returned with a gravity of tone that made Stephanie feel vaguely uncomfortable.

Three days later she wrote Leila a formal note containing her acceptance of the Shakespearean part. Rather to her disappointment, Leila promptly responded with an equally formal note of thanks, and a brief request that she report at the theatre at one o'clock the following Saturday afternoon for a reading of the drama to be later enacted. Stephanie had hoped that Leila would again come to her room, having decided upon a certain lofty pose which she intended to assume during the call. She was also desirous of learning whether Miss Ogden had been included in the cast, an inclusion against which she had determined politely to protest. She had resolved to make life miserable for the offending freshman to the point of driving her from Hamilton College, provided she could accomplish such a revenge. If she could not, it would not be from lack of trying. A pampered only child, Stephanie had grown to young womanhood with a fixed idea of her own importance. Nor was anyone permitted long to stand in her way, whom she could succeed in ousting from it.

Her attendance of the reading of the play at the Playhouse on the following Saturday afternoon revealed to her the not unwelcome fact that Miss Ogden was missing from the cast. It would save her the necessity of a protest, which, she had sulkily reflected, might have reacted to her disadvantage. She was full of secret satisfaction over the good fortune that had visited her, vanity prompting her to repudiate Laura's blunt surmise of how it had come about.

The swift passing of the autumn days found her strictly upon her most gracious behavior toward Leila, Vera and the other members of the cast. Leslie she could not endure. Fortunately for her she seldom came into contact with the busy, reserved manager. Leslie had become everything to the charming little theatre from manager to property man. While Leila directed and rehearsed the actors with unfailing patience and good nature, Leslie was frequently a silent observer at rehearsals. Seated far back in the auditorium little that went on on the stage escaped her critical eyes.

There had been no need for Stephanie to be dissatisfied with her several costumes. In presenting the theatre to the campus Peter Cairns had shown lavish generosity in the matter of wardrobe. He had also placed a costume fund at Leila's disposal to be used at her discretion. The love of acting being a part of Stephanie's vain make-up, she did well in the stellar role of king. She had every reason to be happy, in the new pleasant environment which the rehearsals furnished, but was not. She continued to nurse her grudge against Jewel Ogden, never, for a moment relenting toward the despised freshman.

As a result of the quarrel at the frolic Jewel was still very sore at heart. She had girlishly admired Stephanie for her good looks and imperial manner, and had been cut to the quick by the latter's harsh treatment of herself. She had mentally dwelt upon the disaster to Stephanie's hopes, that she had grown pitifully sensitive. She kept it well hidden, however, under her usual brisk, out-spoken manner. Leslie alone understood that the little girl had not yet emerged from her valley of humiliation. Following her vehement grief on the night of the frolic she had afterward become mute on the subject of her wrongs, refusing to volunteer another word relative to them. Leslie, sympathetically silent, had asked no question.

Leila had already approached Jewel on the subject of her new play, "The Leprachaun," to be enacted later in the college year. This with a view toward "making honors even" and as an indication to Miss Ogden of the impartiality of her policy, germane to matters theatrical. The freshman had accepted the stellar part in the new play which was still engaging Leila's serious literary effort. The Irish girl had determined to make the fanciful drama the best she had yet written. She had carefully explained to Jewel how much the quaint Irish play meant to her, and Jewel had, for the time, emerged from under her secret cloud to brighten over the flattering prospect ahead of her. Later, she dropped again into her former half despondent mood, a change which Leslie quickly noted.

"Cheer up, Jewel, and come on over to Baretti's to dinner. I feel like changing my eats tonight. You eata da spaghet?" She paused before Jewel in droll imitation of Signor Baretti, the friendly proprietor of the restaurant.

"Yes, I do. I love Italian cooking." Jewel's sober face lightened.

"Fine business." Leslie whisked the little girl into her coat before she had time to change her mind, dropping her small felt hat gently on the curly black head.

They were presently seated at an alcove table of the quaint inn, ordering a full Italian dinner that began with Baretti's special snappy relish and would end with Spumoni ice cream and delicious Italian cake. It was still early for the usual nightly throng of college diners at the inn. Besides Leslie and Jewel the tables showed not more than a sprinkling of students, none of whom either girl knew other than by sight. They had just begun their dessert when a party of students entered the restaurant to an accompanying ripple of noise and laughter.

"Oh." Jewel's dessert spoon struck her plate with a nervous little clang as she recognized in the entrants a part of Stephanie Norris's pals, together with Mildred Ferguson. Stephanie, however, was not among them.

They seated themselves at a not far distant table in a laughing flutter, their eyes busily roving the great room.

"I've finished my dessert," Jewel's face had suddenly lost its brightness. "Let's go, Leslie," she entreated.

"We will soon," Leslie nodded, "but we are not going to run away because of that crowd. I refuse to be cheated of my coffee, and you haven't yet taken a sip of yours."

"I don't want it. I'd rather go. Those girls—you don't understand," she declared sadly. "They—that Miss Ferguson—she has said hateful things about me. If we stay she will begin talking about me, and the others will stare at me, and laugh among themselves. I can't bear it." Her red underlip had begun to tremble.

"Steady, kid. Pay no attention to them." Leslie sent a coolly appraising glance at the tableful of girls that was not without its effect. The staring process had already covertly begun, but more than one pair of eyes wavered from the challenging inquiry of her black eyes. The group turned attention to the ordering of their dinner with a promptness that brought the semblance of a grim smile to Leslie's lips.

"What has Miss Ferguson been saying about you?" was Leslie's first question, when ten minutes later, the two girls had stepped out into the soft fall darkness.

"The same sort of things Miss Norris said to me in the gym when I spoiled her dress," quavered Jewel.

"You are positive that she has said them? You know, don't you, that campus gossip is anything but reliable? Remarks often become badly twisted on the way around," Leslie made dry assertion.

"Yes; I know she has. Miss Felton heard her say something unkind about me to Miss Mayhew the other day and censured her for it. I've heard of things she has said from two other freshmen, too. They advised me to go to her and have it out with her. I'd rather not do it. I'm not afraid, but it seems more dignified to ignore her hatefulness, if I can. I made one mistake in answering Miss Norris on the night at the frolic, I don't care to make a second."

"You have the right idea. Stick to it. No one but yourself can make, or mar you." Unconsciously Leslie repeated the very words she had said on a certain spring night of the previous year when a bevy of girls, headed by Mildred Ferguson, had arrayed itself against her.

"That's the way I think, too. You can see for yourself how much better it was not to let it be known on the campus that I used to be a trapeze performer," Jewel said soberly. "I'd have been talked over and sneered at until I'd have been glad to leave Hamilton."

"Not by the girls who count as representative of Hamilton," Leslie sturdily disagreed. "You've lost your nerve. Find it again, and don't let the hissing of these geese worry you."

"I'll try to find it again." Jewel gave a little half-hearted laugh. "Just the same I'm glad only you know about my stage days. You—you're sure you never mentioned it, even to Miss Harper?" Jewel's voice rose anxiously.

"Certainly not; even though I had, you'd still be safe," Leslie humorously assured. "She's an even better secret-keeper than I."

Long after lights were out that night and Jewel slept, vastly comforted by Leslie's kindly effort to cheer her up, Leslie lay wide-awake, pondering a summary method of interference in the freshman's behalf against the persecution of Mildred Ferguson's gossiping tongue. She finally dropped to sleep without having hit upon a decided scheme of action, though daylight and waking would again renew her thoughtful consideration of the problem.

CHAPTER XX

LE PETIT OISEAU

"You are positive of it, Marylyn?" Stephanie Norris's voice betrayed triumphant excitement. "You must be able to prove, you know, that she really *is* the person you saw in Paris, before you dare let the news get out on the campus. Otherwise she would fly at you like a hornet, or else take her troubles to Prexy."

"I'm positive enough of what I tell you. I can prove it, too, by a French theatre program I have with her picture on the front cover. I have always been puzzled, wondering why her face seemed so familiar to me. I was sure I'd seen her somewhere on the Continent when we were abroad last summer. The night of the frolic I was more sure of it than ever when I saw her in that peachblow frock, doing that fancy trot with the tall soph. Even then I couldn't place her. Yesterday afternoon I was talking to Miss Werner who was in Paris about the same time that we were. We both happened to remember a particularly good vaudeville show we'd seen there. Then it flashed across me, all of a sudden, '*Le Petit Oiseau.*' That's the way she was programmed. She came out first in a dress that was almost the same shade of pink as the one she wore to the frolic, and did some marvelously clever acrobatic stunts. Then she changed to a scarlet and black trapeze rig with cunning little black wings. She had a partner then, a catcher, I believe they call him, and then she did some toppo stunts on the flying trapeze."

Marylyn Spencer, small, and rather pretty, save for a pair of lynx-like, calculating eyes, fairly paused for breath after her rapidly-spoken revelation. She was a faithful satellite of Stephanie's, far more in harmony with the latter's high-handed methods than was Laura. "I've written to Mother to send me the program. It was so artistic I kept it as a Paris souvenir. I know I'm right about it," she finished emphatically.

"*A common trapeze performer,*" Arline Redmond said with infinite disdain. "*That is* the limit. No wonder she behaved like a wild cat to you at the frolic, Steve. She certainly doesn't belong at Hamilton. There *are* colleges, of course, suited to such *ambitious persons.*" She laughed disagreeably. "She had nerve to come to Hamilton."

"I imagine she got into Hamilton under false pretenses." Stephanie took eager advantage of the opening. "Possibly Miss Cairns may know the truth about her. I'll say the faculty doesn't. When do you expect to receive that program from home, Marylyn?"

"Within three or four days. Why? What are you going to do?" she demanded curiously. More or less of her curiosity was reflected upon the faces of the other girls who were present in Stephanie's room. Among the group Laura alone maintained a bored silence. No word of the gossiping conversation, going on animatedly in the room, was "getting by" her.

"Never mind what I'm going to do. Let me have that program as soon as you can. Then look out." Stephanie gave a soft malicious little laugh.

"You'll have to be very careful what you do, Steve," warned Mildred Ferguson half sourly. She had been unable to "think up" a telling revenge against Jewel Ogden and was slightly peeved at Marylyn's success. "If you start anything about Miss Ogden having been a circus performer going on the campus you'll soon find both Miss Cairns and Miss Harper on your trail. They can make it hot for you, too."

"*That* for Miss Cairns and Miss Harper," Stephanie snapped contemptuous fingers. "Miss Harper is lovely to me, and Miss Cairns would be, too, if I gave her the slightest opening. Don't worry, I know how to put this little stunt over, and no one, outside you girls here, will be able to say how it happened."

"Much ado about nothing," Laura had come out of her bored silence. "Possibly, after Steve has behaved like the villain in a melodrama you'll then all discover that the Ogden kid doesn't care a hang who knows she was once a trapeze performer. It may give her a fine boost on the campus."

"Nothing of the sort." Stephanie turned angrily upon Laura. "If she'd felt like that about it she would have boasted of it long ago, to me. She's horribly conceited. No, indeed. She was always very evasive whenever I happened to ask her any personal questions. Besides, she told me she had attended Warburton Prep."

"Possibly she had," Laura retorted.

"I doubt it. You're always on the wrong side of the fence lately. Since you don't agree with me, please, at least, remember that this is a confidential talk," Stephanie reminded icily.

"Now you *have* said something." Laura thereupon subsided with an amused air which only an odd glint in her pale blue eyes contradicted.

Meanwhile Jewel had taken Leslie's blunt advice to heart and was trying to regain the self-assured air that had characterized her during her first days at college. Hearing no further adverse criticisms of herself she was now glad that she had followed the line of conduct which Leslie had advocated.

Returning from a ride with Leslie in the late October dusk the eyes of both girls were simultaneously attracted by the sight of a folded newspaper held in place by the knob of their room door.

"The Hamilton Gazette," Jewel read in surprise. "How queer, and it's addressed to me! I wonder who put it there?"

"Some little mystery." Leslie had already entered the room and switched on the light. Her thoughts elsewhere, she was paying no particular attention to the freshman as she stood ripping off the news sheet's addressed wrapper. She heard, mechanically, the rustle of unfolding paper, followed by sudden silence.

"Oh-h-h-h!"

Leslie was unprepared for the long, anguished wail which Jewel sent up. Sight of the little girl's horrified expression, and she came quickly forward, saying anxiously, "What's the matter, Jewel?"

"Read it! Read it!" the freshman cried, holding the paper toward Leslie with shaking hands. "Look. *You* did that. No one but you could have done it. I— I—hate you!" She thrust the paper forcefully into Leslie's hands.

"What?" Leslie had already busied herself with the fateful news sheet. Squarely at top center of the first page was a badly-blurred picture of a girl in a very short-skirted evening frock. Her pose, however, was distinctly theatrical. Despite blurred reproduction the girl in the picture was unmistakably Jewel. Below the picture Leslie read the large-type headline, "Trapeze Performer a College Innovation."

Amazed interest glued Leslie's eyes to the half column article below the head line. She read on, dimly conscious of Jewel's accompanying angry voice.

"Where did you get that picture?" she finished in time to hear Jewel storm. "You had it all the time. You must have seen our show in Paris, then pretended innocence to me. That picture was on the theatre program, and you know it. No one else knew about me except you. How *could* you?"

"Come out of it, Jewel," Leslie said with brusque kindness. "Listen to me. Didn't I give you my word of honor regarding your secret?"

"Yes, and broke it," Jewel flung back furiously.

"You should know me better than that. Try to be reasonable. What object would I possibly have in doing any such contemptible thing?"

"How should I know? Probably you told your friend Mrs. Macy about it. She may have told another of her intimate friends," Jewel replied bitterly. "She— "

"I have told *no one*. Mrs. Macy is above reproach. You will kindly leave her name out of the discussion." Pale with wrath, the chill of Leslie's tones cut through Jewel's anger.

"Perhaps she didn't—" she began, half ashamed; Leslie, however, had reached the door and left the room without heeding the angry freshman's half attempt at exoneration. Left to herself resentment against Leslie again possessed her. When, half an hour later, Leslie returned, well over the surge of black anger that had threatened to burst upon Jewel, the freshman appeared stonily unaware of her presence in the room.

In the dining room that evening girl comment ran decorously rife. Every freshie at the Hall had found a copy of the "Hamilton Gazette" at her door that afternoon. They awaited Jewel's entrance into the dining room with more or less eager curiosity. She did not appear at dinner, to their signal disappointment. Far from being shocked at the write-up, the broader-minded element among them were inclined to lionize Jewel. Weighed down by a false sense of shame, she could not possibly guess this.

In Stephanie Norris's room that evening a triumphantly lively discussion went on at Stephanie's coup de grace. The freshman's non-appearance at dinner they had chose to regard as significant.

"I knew I was right about her," Marylyn Spencer elatedly repeated. "However did you manage, Steve? I mean so that there won't be a come-back for you. Remember I must have that program back again."

"I'm going into town tomorrow. I'll send a messenger boy from the Hamilton House for it, and wait for its return to me there. I shall simply tell him," Stephanie broke into an amused laugh, "to ask the editor for Miss Harper's program."

"Miss Harper?" went up in several different keys of surprise.

"Yes. It's awfully funny. You see I happened to mention Miss Harper's name in connection with the Playhouse, and the editor must have mistaken me for her. He very politely called me Miss Harper. So—" again she laughed,—"I let it go at that."

"Then, no one can possibly connect us with—" Joyce Gray, Marylyn's roommate began excitedly.

"This pleasant little joke," Laura Taylor supplied mockingly. "You were in luck again, weren't you, Steve."

"Yes." Stephanie cast a suspicious glance at Laura. The latter's immobile face told her nothing.

"I imagine she will try to brave this out," Mildred Ferguson said half contemptuously. "Some of the students are silly enough to begin making a fuss over her. We ought to do something more, before this affair dies out, to chase her off the campus."

"What?" came in an expectant chorus.

"Haze her," Mildred replied very deliberately.

"It's strictly forbidden at Hamilton," demurred Edith Barber. "It's sure enough expellment if one is caught at it."

"Oh, yes, of course, but one needn't be caught at it. I know something we might do that couldn't possibly be proven against us, if we were to be caught hazing that midget. Are you willing to try it out?"

"I am," Stephanie made instant reply.

"I'd rather know what your plan is before making any promises," Joyce said doubtfully.

"So should I," came from two or three of the others.

"Never mind, I'll tell you about it, then you can decide," Mildred conceded. "There's a room at the back of Hamilton Hall, first floor, that the students are permitted to use for rehearsals of campus house plays. All one has to do is to ask the janitor for the key, and it can be entered from a side door. The door opening upon the corridor can be locked. All one has to promise is to be out of the room by ten o'clock. First we'll write Miss Ogden a note asking her to come to that room by the side entrance at eight o'clock on a certain evening for the discussion of a grave matter. We'll simply sign it 'Chairman, Senior Welfare Committee.' When she steps into the room she'll see seven masked figures in gray dominos waiting for her. One of us, it had better be Steve, will play chairman and make her a speech about campus interests demanding that she leave Hamilton. Steve will have to speak very sternly, so as to make her believe that she is really in bad with the best class of Hamilton students because of the write-up in the 'Gazette.' Nine chances out of ten she will swallow the bait and leave college. None of the rest of us will say a word, and Steve will have to disguise her voice. If anyone should happen to be around that might make trouble we can easily explain our presence there by saying we were simply rehearsing a little play, and deny knowing anything about either the note we'll send her, or the Senior Welfare Committee. But there's absolutely no danger of discovery." Mildred glanced about the circle of interested faces, confident that she had scored.

"It's a dandy scheme." Stephanie drew a long breath of satisfaction. "But I can't disguise my voice well enough to act as chairman. Laura can." She looked dubiously at her roommate, not sure but that Laura would balk. "Would you be the chairman, Laura?" she asked persuasively.

"Yes." Laura's prompt acceptance made Stephanie open her eyes.

"I'll write you a speech. You'll have to learn it by heart and practice it," Mildred told the stout freshman. "It ought to be something like this: 'My dear Miss Ogden, it has long been the custom of a selected committee of seniors, secretly appointed each year by a certain person to deal privately with such matters as may rise to interfere with the welfare of the students of Hamilton.' How is that?" she appealed, laughing.

"Fine," exulted Stephanie.

An accompanying murmur of approval arose. Laura alone kept silence.

"What do you think of it, Laura?" Stephanie was aware of Laura's muteness.

"It will answer the purpose. When will the party come off, where are the dominos to come from?"

"We'll buy the cloth and make them. We can run them up by hand tomorrow night. I'll make yours for you while you're learning your part. I'll write the speech this very night. This is Tuesday. We can try our little stunt on Thursday, provided no one else is going to use the room on Thursday night. I'll find that out tomorrow morning. The sooner it happens, the sooner we'll see the last of Jewel Marie Ogden."

CHAPTER XXI

ALL IN THE NAME OF WELFARE

"Suppose she shouldn't come?" Behind the gray of her mask Joyce Rawlston gave a faint giggle.

"She will, I think," Mildred Ferguson predicted. "I heard today that she was all broke-up over the write-up. She has been taking her meals at Baretti's, too. That's why we haven't seen her in the dining room at the Hall."

"It's a wonder Miss Cairns hasn't been trotting around with her, trying to show how much democracy she has," Marylyn Spencer curled a red upper lip. "They've not been seen together since the afternoon when the story came out in the 'Gazette.'"

"Miss Cairns is looking after her own interests by dropping her, I presume. She had better watch her step. She used to be considered the most lawless student that ever enrolled at Hamilton. She made a wise change in her ways when she managed to get back again on the campus. Now she plumes herself on being so intimate with Marjorie Dean Macy and that crowd of wonder workers. I *detest* Leslie Cairns," Mildred exclaimed with bitter energy.

"For goodness' sake, Laura, don't fall down on your speech," Stephanie interposed nervously. She was tired of hearing Mildred's tirade against Leslie, from a too frequent repetition of it.

"I won't. Let me alone," Laura replied to Stephanie in the deep forbidding voice she was soon to use as chairman.

"Will she knock on the door?" Reba Franklin cast a quick glance toward the appointed portal by which Jewel Marie Ogden must enter, provided she obeyed the dread summons.

"No. The note directed her to open the door, and walk in. Sh-h-h. I'm sure I heard a step," Mildred raised a warning finger.

Came the turn of the knob. A muffled sigh ascended from the masked tribunal. Jewel Ogden had stepped into the room, her black eyes fixed upon the waiting gray dominos in an expression of anxious dread. For an instant she stood poised on the threshold as though about to turn and flee, then she came slowly forward until she was within a few feet of the long oak bench on which were seated the fearsome company of masks.

"I received a note," she began bravely, "from the Chairman of the Campus Welfare Committee. I should like to speak to her, please." Her eyes roved timidly up and down the line of masks.

"I am the chairman." Laura had risen. She stepped forward a little, standing between the diminutive freshman and the row of silent dominos. "My dear Miss Ogden," she began, "it has long been the custom in almost every college for the unjust to persecute the just. You have been summoned here tonight by a certain group of girls who have yet to learn how to live, or how to let others live."

"Oh-h! Oh-h! Why, the idea!" The impressiveness of the masked figures had been suddenly lost in the angry babble of girl voices that rose from behind the gray masks.

"*Silence.*" The sternness of the command, spoken in a voice that was certainly not Laura Taylor's, pre-empted an odd uncomfortable hush. "*I* am the chairman of this committee, and I am going to deliver a speech suitable to the occasion. It will not be a long speech, but it will be strictly to the point. It seems hardly necessary for me to inform you students that you are hazing. It is a dangerous pastime on Hamilton campus."

"You are not Laura Taylor!" Stephanie had sprung angrily to her feet. "You have no right to be here spying upon us."

"What right have you to be here in the existing circumstances?" lashed out the stern voice.

"We are—we are going to rehearse a play," Stephanie declared defiantly.

"Not now; the show is over, and the play is played out."

"We had permission to use this room this evening. You are intruding." Mildred Ferguson had rallied stormily to Stephanie's aid.

"Very true, Miss Ferguson, but, circumstances alter cases. I came here tonight to see that Miss Ogden received fair treatment. Also to say to you that hazing does not pay; neither does spite and malice. I tried them all once, here at Hamilton, so I know now that advice to you is sound."

"Leslie Cairns," Mildred Ferguson almost shouted out the name.

"Yes; Leslie Cairns, the most lawless student who ever enrolled at Hamilton College." As she spoke Leslie threw back the hood of the domino and stripped the mask from her face. "I'm trying now to live down that reputation. I *was* expelled, you see. You have merely run the risk, but it's a bad risk to run."

"*Laura,*" gasped Marylyn, "Where is she? She's to blame for—" she checked herself.

"Yes; she is. She came to me in confidence today because she had the courage of her convictions. She wishes you to know this; asked me to tell you. That's all, I believe. Come on. Jewel, let's go over to Baretti's for ice cream. Good night, masks. The next time you decide to start on a student you don't happen to fancy, think it over, and don't start."

Her arm linked in Jewel's, the tiny girl had begun to cry, quietly, pitifully, she drew her freshie catch toward the door, leaving an oddly silent row of chagrined girls behind them.

CHAPTER XXII

GOLDENDEDE'S CHOICE

That which Jewel had so greatly feared proved itself to be instead the beginning of her rise in campus popularity. Her tearful apologies to Leslie the latter met with a smiling "Forget it." Deciding to do some investigating on her own account, Leslie took occasion to drop into the "Gazette" one afternoon for an interview with the editor. She came out of the office laughing immoderately and drove post haste for Wayland Hall.

"Do you know yet who furnished the paper with that program and write-up?" she asked Jewel as she came breezily into their room.

"No; you know I don't. Of course I suspect Miss Norris of it, and of course I can't prove it." Jewel could now afford to smile at the matter. She was tasting the sweetness of being valued at last for having achieved for herself an international fame as Le Petit Oiseau.

"Do you care now who did it?" Leslie questioned shrewdly.

"No; not now, except to be glad that I've no tiresome secret to bother me."

"All right. Then I'll tell you who did it. It was Leila Harper."

"*Oh, no,*" Jewel cried out in protest.

"Yes." Leslie's sober features broke up in laughter. "Oh, Kid, you must let me tell it to Leila. She's due to get a shock. That spite-chaser, Miss Norris, gave the editor of the 'Gazette' the impression that she was Miss Harper. I nearly dropped when he shot it at me. Then I guilefully drew him into giving me a description of Miss Harper, and he described Miss Norris instead."

"Go and tell her," Jewel gave laughing permission. "Tell her *everything.*"

"Now would not that discourage even an Irish playwright?" was Leila's droll reception of the news of her supposed perfidy. "I am no villain, but it seems I swank as one in editors' offices. I shall warn Vera against myself. Even now I may be conniving against her, and that without even poor Midget suspecting me. Oh, wurra, wurra!"

Leslie presently left Leila, her face bright with recollection of the Irish girl's warm commendation. She had, partly by chance, partly by determined resolve, managed to strike a telling blow for democracy. She and Laura Taylor had also made a pact toward reclaiming Stephanie Norris from the narrowness of her snobbish ways. On returning to her room on the night of the frustrated attempt at hazing, Stephanie had sat down and cried, saying she was not sorry the plan had failed, and blaming Mildred Ferguson for proposing it in the beginning. Toward Laura she had even exhibited an oddly grudging respect.

While Leslie trod the trail of democracy, Marjorie continued to help Miss Susanna hunt for the secret drawer. Miss Hamilton had received but one brief letter from Peter Cairns in which he wrote that he had, as yet, nothing of special importance to report in regard to Lawyer Norris.

"Why, oh, why, can't that miserable secret drawer open like magic, and show itself?" grumbled Miss Susanna one November afternoon following a fresh going over of the Chinese room. "I shan't waste any more time in this room. I don't believe he ever put those papers in here. Did he?" she inquired of a squat, severe-visaged Chinese idol that stood on top of a teakwood cabinet. "*You* wouldn't tell me, if you could speak." She pointed an accusing finger at the squatting god.

"Could it possibly be anywhere in Mr. Brooke's bedroom?" Marjorie said speculatively. "We've never hunted much for it in there."

"Let's go up there and see what we may see. It wouldn't have been like him, though, to keep his papers there," the old lady said a trifle wearily.

"Leila said we'd some day find it in the last place we might guess," Marjorie reminded cheerfully. She understood that Miss Hamilton's disappointment at not having found the drawer was weighing heavily upon her.

The large square, airy chamber that had once been Brooke Hamilton's contained few pieces of furniture. A four-poster mahogany bed, a highboy, a chest of drawers, one or two tables, three chairs and a night stand beside the bed completed the furnishings with the exception of one other bit of furniture. It was a plain, square-topped stand of shining mahogany that stood in a large bow window. Marjorie knew it to be Angela Vernon's workstand. Miss Susanna had told her its pathetic history. Angela's brother had given it to Brooke Hamilton as a memento of his fiancee soon after Angela's sudden death. It contained bright silks and wools which she had loved to fashion into gifts for her dear ones, as well as an unfinished bit of embroidery and still another of fairy-like tatting.

Marjorie had once before begun a gentle search in the body of the stand, the top of which lifted. Miss Susanna had discouraged further search by declaring that there was no likelihood of finding it there. Entering the room of the departed master of Hamilton Arms that sunny afternoon the slowly descending sunlight in the west seemed to point golden fingers at the little stand.

"I'm going to look in the little stand again, Goldendede," she called while Miss Susanna began a fussy ransacking of the highboy.

"Very well, but it's a forlorn hope."

Marjorie smiled to herself as she raised the lid of the stand and applied careful hands to the old-time handiwork of Brooke Hamilton's sweetheart. Bereft of its treasures the two bare compartments of the stand showed no promise of either a secret compartment, or drawer.

She returned the contents with a little romantic breath. It would be fitting, she thought, to have found the drawer in the dear, cunning stand, once Angela Vernon's.

"Nothing." She shook her curly head as Miss Susanna glanced inquiringly toward her.

"No; it's not much more than a toy stand, Marjorie. Would you mind moving it over here. It used always to be in the corner on the left of Uncle Brooke's bed."

"It's heavier than one might believe," Marjorie said as she grasped it firmly by the two front corners and lifted it. Of a sudden she heard an odd, whirring sound, something shot out of the stand, striking her smartly against the knees, sending her staggering backward. She uttered a startled cry as her downward glance caught the white of neatly-folded papers reposing in orderly fashion in a shallow drawer that had sprung open from the lower part of the box-like square which formed the compartments.

"Child, child," Miss Susanna had now dropped to the floor and sat hugging the paper-filled little drawer. "There was a false bottom to that stand, and I never even suspected it. It belonged to Angela Vernon's great-grand-mother. Those were the palmy days of such secret devices. How ever did you happen to hit upon the mechanism?"

"I don't know. I might ask however did the mechanism happen to hit me?" Marjorie returned, face glowing with the happiness of the unexpected discovery.

"We'll take the drawer to the study at once and go over these papers. Come along, Chickie." Miss Susanna started from the room with a degree of triumphant briskness.

"Just as I imagined," she said an hour later as she laid the penned agreement made between her kinsman and Lawyer Norris upon the table. "This agreement distinctly specifies that, in the event of Uncle Brooke's death, I was then to be apprised of this agreement and, also, that the privilege of choosing 'the one' was to be mine after I had reached the age of eighteen.

Norris was to receive two thousand dollars a year for his services. The fifty thousand dollar check was deposited in the Surety Trust Bank of New York City. Now we shall make headway. I shall write Peter to come here at once. With the actual facts now at our command we shall be able to trace Norris's movements, and learn what became of him and his trust after Uncle died."

"Dear, dear Goldendede," Marjorie rubbed a soft cheek against the old lady's wrinkled one, "I'd rather not be the one. Please choose Leila instead. She's done such splendid work for Hamilton."

"It can't be done, Marjorie." The shadow of a frown touched Miss Hamilton's brows. "You are the 'one' in the sense Uncle Brooke dreamed of; Leila is a splendid girl; a genius. Still she came to Hamilton a whole year before you came, accomplishing nothing beyond success in her college studies. Suppose I were to choose her as the 'one' I should meet with plenty of dissenters. Suppose I should name you. I shall, you know. No use in trying to escape me. The whole college would rise up and call me level-headed. You understand now what I mean?"

"Yes; but there's my side, too, to consider. You must understand the way I feel about it," Marjorie gently argued.

"You've often said you wished to try to carry on even a small part of Uncle Brooke's work at Hamilton. Because you have been a devoted friend to his college you are chosen to enrich it by fifty thousand dollars. Isn't that worth the great discomfort of having been chosen by me as the 'One'?" There was a hint of growing irritation in the old lady's question. She resented being crossed in so important a matter even by Marjorie.

"It's not a great discomfort—only—. It's not the glory of having worked for Hamilton that I care about. It's the work itself I glory in. I wish to carry on Mr. Brooke's work still, whenever I can. Couldn't we have a very private presentation, Goldendede, with only you and Prexy, and the girls and a few other of my close friends in attendance?" she put wistfully.

"No; we couldn't." Miss Susanna laid the paper she had been examining on the table with an irritated little flip. "We may not have it at all," she snapped as she hustled toward the door.

Marjorie heard the door close behind the old lady. She looked up with a brave, but rueful face at the portrait on the wall. "I'm sorry, but I don't wish to be the one; not even a tiny bit," she said childishly aloud.

"I had to come back, dear child," Miss Susanna had softly opened the door in time to hear Marjorie's sober comment. "Forgive this old crosspatch. Here is the letter he wrote Lawyer Norris that has shown me strongly how much his heart was in the idea of the Honor Fund, and the One. Read it."

Silence settled down in the sun-bright study as youth and age sat reading the words of one long passed. Finally Marjorie laid down the bulky letter she had just finished. "You win," she nodded to the portrait.

CHAPTER XXIII

LEILA FINDS ROMANCE

"You've done wonders, Peter. The secret drawer furnished us with the facts, but it took you to hunt down Norris's son, and trace the check after it fell into the son's hands. That rascal should be brought to book for appropriating that check and building up a fortune from it. You say he is now worth half a million." Miss Susanna pursed her lips, shaking her head, "He's a rascal," she repeated, "Half a million, Hm-m."

"He's rated at that." There was an odd light in Peter Cairns' black eyes, and an enigmatic smile played about his lips. "I have a few surprises up my sleeve," he told the same interested little company that had sat with him in the library on his latest visit at the Arms.

"If you've one for me, ready," Hal had assumed a listening attitude.

"This same Norris who appropriated the fifty thousand dollar check owns those properties you wish to buy. I have arranged to take them over for you at your own figure."

"Tell me nothing." Hal borrowed one of Leila's pet surprise phrases.

"This will interest you," he nodded to Leslie, Leila and Vera. "He has a daughter at Hamilton in the freshman class. I suppose you know her?" he interrogated.

"Yes." Blank surprise flashed over the faces of the trio as they nodded affirmative.

"What sort of girl is she—clever, or stupid?" he inquired pointedly.

"She is clever at acting. She's to play King Hal in our production of 'Henry the Fifth,'" Leila informed him.

"I have heard that she made brilliant recitations," Leslie conceded.

"She is really a beautiful girl," Vera remarked after a moment of silence.

"I'm going to ask Leslie a question," Peter Cairns smiled fondly at his daughter. "What would you think of me if I had done what Norris has done in the matter of appropriating this check for his own use?"

"I don't know. I couldn't bear it. Try to be honest always, won't you, Peter?" The intensity with which Leslie began her reply lightened into a rather wavery chuckle.

"Oh, ha, ha!" Vastly amused at Leslie's reply, the financier continued, "It's like this. I've had it out with Norris about everything. He is willing to make good the fifty thousand dollar check. He admits that he did wrong in not communicating with Miss Susanna soon after Mr. Brooke's death. His father died shortly before Mr. Brooke. He also admitted to me that he had hoped his daughter might win the honor fund when she should be of an age to enter Hamilton. He suspected that Miss Susanna knew little or nothing about the arrangement, since she had never tried to get into touch with him. He decided to hold back the fund for his daughter's benefit. He had heard a good deal about Marjorie as a shining light at Hamilton, but he believed his daughter might go her one better. It took time and patience to get these unlovely facts from him, but I persevered with him and got them. He understands that his position is serious. He is willing to make any amend he can, financial or other, because of his love for his daughter. He wishes her never to know that he has been other than above reproach. You have the facts. What shall you do about him, Miss Susanna?"

"Oh, let the rascal go, for his daughter's sake. Make him turn over those Kenton Street properties to Marjorie's colony," was the old lady's disgusted mandate. "You settle the whole matter with him, Peter. I rely upon you implicitly. So glad you and Leslie are soon coming to the Hedge. I shall make good use of my new neighbors." She chuckled at her own joke.

"Three cheers for Goldendede, who can show us all a lesson in magnificent magnanimity." Leslie was on her feet, her dark eyes beaming admiring affection of Miss Susanna.

The room rang with the happy sound of voices raised in honor of Miss Susanna's kindly decision. Then they all took hands and indulged in a joyful little prance about the pleased old lady. Jonas, coming to the doorway all smiles was seized and whisked into the laughing, gyrating circle.

"Come and sing us a French song, Leslie," coaxed Vera, a little later as the talk fell away from the all-important subject of the honor fund to drift into lighter, happier channels. As she spoke, Vera had begun to tow Leslie toward the library door.

In the music room Leila found herself sitting a little away from the piano, talking rather self-consciously to Peter Cairns.

"Leslie told me something you once said to her, Leila," Peter Cairns said with his usual abruptness, "which amused me so much I must ask you about it."

"What was that?" Leila inquired curiously.

"It was about that prospective bridegroom of yours, the old man with the white hair whom you might boss unmercifully." The financier's lips were smiling, but his dark eyes were fixed purposefully upon the Irish girl's features.

"Ah, yes." Leila could not repress an enjoying grin. "I have not yet found him."

"I wish I had his qualifications to the dot. I haven't. I'm not yet a snowy-haired monument to old age, but I have at least one of them, I am willing to be bossed unmercifully."

Blue eyes met black squarely, a faint flush crept into Leila's cheeks, then the ridiculousness of the conversation being borne upon them both they burst into laughter.

"Seriously, Leila," Peter Cairns had changed again from laughter to purpose, "won't you think about what I've said?"

"I will think about it," Leila promised. Her eyes had an absent mystic light in their depths.

"I love you, Leila," he said again, "I've loved you almost from the day I first met you."

"I will think about that, too," she returned soberly, and for a brief instant she permitted his strong brown fingers to close over her own.

THE END

Lightning Source UK Ltd.
Milton Keynes UK
UKHW010745271222
414464UK00004B/305